SMART

MUM

SMART

Colin
X

KIM
SLATER

MACMILLAN
CHILDREN'S BOOKS

First published 2014 by Macmillan Children's Books
a division of Macmillan Publishers Limited
20 New Wharf Road, London N1 9RR
Basingstoke and Oxford
Associated companies throughout the world
www.panmacmillan.com

ISBN 978-1-4472-5409-6

1 3 5 7 9 8 6 4 2

A CIP catalogue record for this book is available from
the British Library.

Printed and bound by CPI Group (UK) Ltd, Croydon CR0 4YY

To Mackie, Francesca Kim and Mama

'I am a simple man' L. S. Lowry

①

DEAD IN THE WATER

It just looked like a pile of rags, floating on the water.

Jean sat on the bench with the brass plaque on. It said: *In Memory of Norman Reeves, who spent many happy hours here.*

The plaque means Norman Reeves is dead, but it doesn't actually say that.

Jean held her head in her hands and her body was all jerky, like when you are laughing or crying. I guessed she was crying and I was right.

'He was my friend,' she sobbed.

I looked around but Jean was alone. People around here say Jean is 'cuckoo'. That means mental. She used to be a nurse that delivered babies. She still knows loads of stuff she learned from medical books but no one believes her.

'Who?' I asked.

Jean pointed to the rags.

I went to the edge of the embankment to look. There was a stripy bag half in the water. I saw a face with a bushy beard in the middle of the rags, under the ripples. One eye was open, one was closed.

I freaked out. The sea sound started in my head and I ran right past the bridge and back again but there was nobody to help. I'm not supposed to run like mad because it can start my asthma off.

'When the sea noise comes in your head,' Miss Crane says, 'it is important to stay calm and breathe.'

I stopped running. I tried to stay calm and breathe. I used my inhaler.

Jean was still crying when I got back.

'He was my friend,' she said again. I picked up a long stick and took it over to the riverbank. I poked at the face but not near the eyes.

'What are you doing?' Jean shouted from the bench.

'I'm doing a test to see if it's a balloon,' I yelled back. It felt puffy and hard at the same time, so I knew it was Jean's friend's head.

'Is it a balloon?' shouted Jean.

A woman with a dog was coming.

When she got near I said, 'Jean's friend is in the river.'

She gave me a funny look, like she might ignore me and carry on walking. Then she came a bit nearer and looked at the river. She started screaming.

I went for a walk up the embankment to stay calm and breathe. Some Canada geese flew down and skidded into the water. They didn't care about the rags and the puffy face. They just got on with it.

When I got back, a policeman and a policewoman were talking to the lady with the dog. Jean was still sitting on the bench but nobody was talking to her.

'That's him,' the woman said, and pointed at me.

'What's your name, son?' The policeman asked.

'I'm not your son,' I said. 'My dad is dead from a disease that made him drink cider, even in the morning.'

The policeman and the policewoman looked at each other.

'Can you tell us what happened, love?' The policewoman had a kind face, like Mum when she wasn't rushing to go to work. She nodded her head towards the river. 'Is that how you found him?'

'It looked like rags,' I said.

'He was my friend,' Jean shouted from the bench.

The policewoman wrote down my name and address.

'Was he just like this, when you got here?' asked the policeman.

'The head was a bit more turned towards the bridge,' I said. 'Before I poked it with the stick.'

'Stick?'

'I had to see if it was a balloon or a real head,' I said.

The woman with the dog shrieked. She even made the policewoman jump.

'It's definitely a real head,' I said.

'Did you see anyone else around here but the tramp lady?' asked the policeman.

'Jean was a nurse,' I said. 'She's not mental.'

A white van pulled up. It had the words *Police Diving Unit* on the side and a blue flashing light. Even when it stood still, the light kept flashing.

'Kieran,' said the policeman. 'Did you see anyone else hanging around here?'

'No,' I said. 'How many divers will go in?'

The side of the van slid back and two police divers got out. They had flippers on and everything.

'They'll need breathing apparatus on if they're going to search the water for clues,' I said.

'No need for that,' the policewoman said in a low voice, like she didn't want me to hear. 'Poor old bogger probably fell in after one too many.'

A man got out of the front of the police van and took some photographs of Jean's friend in the water. Then the divers put up some screens while they pulled the body out of the river.

'Why are they hiding it?' I said. 'I've already seen it.'

'And poked it,' said the policeman as they moved away. 'Don't go touching dead bodies in future.'

There were some people gathering on the far bank. One man had binoculars.

The police emptied the dead man's stripy bag and spread the things out on the concrete. There was a blanket, some socks and an empty packet of cheese straws.

Two older boys from my school walked up and stood watching.

'What you been up to, Downs? You topped somebody?' asked one of them.

'I haven't got Down's,' I said. 'There's nothing wrong with my chromosomes.'

'Are you sure about that, Downs?' asked the other boy.

They fell about laughing.

(2)
THE LETTER

One day I'm going to be a reporter for the *Evening Post*. That's why I started walking straight home, so I could write stuff down.

I don't write in my notebook all the time. I used to only write in it when bad things happened, like when Grandma stopped coming round.

But now I write down all the interesting things that happen too, so the Editor of the *Post* will want me to work for him when I leave school. I can show him my notebook as evidence of my reporting skills.

The bad thing at the river was definitely interesting.

I can do the tiniest writing in the world; even I can't read it sometimes. Nobody can tell other people what I've said, which is the best thing. You can't trust people but you can trust your notebook.

I ripped out all the pages of my old *Beano* annual and I hide my notebook in there. Then I put the annual in the middle of a pile of other annuals under the bed. Nobody will ever find it.

See, this is why I like writing in my notebook. I can talk about anything that's ever been invented and no one can tell me off.

I. Am. In. Charge.

You can write sentences with only one word in them, like that. It's your choice.

I live in Nottingham. Not right in the middle, where the castle is, just at the edge of the middle.

'Just outside the city centre,' Miss Crane says.

I like saying 'edge of the middle' better. It feels more like a place.

Robin Hood came from Nottingham. He lived in Sherwood Forest and formed a merry band of men, including Little John, who was massive. Yorkshire tried to steal Robin Hood. They said he came from there but it's been proven by scientists that he was from Nottingham.

I stopped walking for a minute and looked back at the embankment and the flashing blue lights of the police van.

Sometimes, when I look at the river I imagine it is a long, thin piece of sea. If you followed it for nearly a year, you could reach Australia. It's been here as long as Robin Hood. He might have stood in some of the exact same places as I do, looking at the river. I said that once, to my older brother.

'Course he did,' he replied. 'You daft prat.'

Ryan is my older brother but not a proper one. I've got a different mum and dad to him.

My dad died. I only know him because of the

photographs that Mum kept to show me. I was just a baby then. Miss Crane says our brains store away everything that's happened to us, but you can't remember everything because some memories get locked up in a bit of your brain you don't use, called the 'subconscious'.

In my subconscious, there are pictures and films of my dad playing with me and tucking me into bed. Nobody can take them away and burn them. I wish I could get them out of my locked bit of brain to look at again.

When I got home I stopped at the living-room door on my way upstairs, but nobody turned round. Mum wasn't back from work yet, so I couldn't tell her about what had happened. Sometimes she leaves for work before I wake up and doesn't come back till after I'm in bed, even on the weekends.

Tony was lying on the settee, smoking, with his eyes nearly closed, and Ryan was playing Call of Duty. The gunfire was very loud. Louder than Mum liked it.

Mum says I have to call Tony 'Dad', but secretly, in my head, I always say 'Tony' straight after, so it cancels it out.

Ryan was supposed to go to college to do Media Studies at the beginning of September. After two days he said he didn't like it, so Tony said he could stop going. After that, he played soldier games all day long and nearly all night. When he went up each wave, he went barmy, like he was a real soldier in Afghanistan.

'Yes! Who's the daddy?' he kept saying and punching my arm.

When you say that, it means you think you're the best of anyone in the whole world at something. Ryan thought he was the best at Call of Duty.

'Dean Shelton in my class is on the last wave,' I told him.

'Shut your mouth,' he yelled. 'Before I bleeping smack you one.'

Writing 'bleep' takes all the power out of swear words.

A long, long time ago, someone decided what word to use for every single thing there is. For a wooden thing you sit on, they decided that word would be CHAIR. But what if they had decided it would be called a B*****D? Then you would sit on a B*****D and call someone a CHAIR if you hated them.

'That's true,' Miss Crane had said when I'd asked her about it at school. 'It's the meaning we attach to a word that's important.'

When I've worked at the *Evening Post* for a bit, I want to go and work for Sky.

Sky is 'First for Breaking News'. All the politicians want to talk to Sky first, even before the BBC.

I like Jeremy Thompson but I don't want to present the news like him. I want to do a job like Martin Brunt.

He's my favourite on the Sky News team.

Martin Brunt is the Crime Correspondent. He comes on when very bad stuff happens, like murders. If he lived around here, he would be down at the river now, reporting back to viewers about Jean's friend, who was dead in the water.

The Sky News cameraman would zoom in on the rags and they'd bring criminal experts into the studio to say what kind of person might have killed the man. The experts are called 'criminologists'. They even know what car the murderer drives and whether he still lives with his mum and dad.

In my room, I wrote down all the evidence I'd seen so far in my notebook. I did it in very small writing so I could fit it all in. 'Evidence' means every single thing that has happened. Sometimes on *CSI*, they don't even realize something is evidence until later on. Then they look at their notes to check it out.

I wrote down all the people I'd seen that morning, even Jean. At this stage, everyone was a suspect. Really, I knew Jean hadn't done anything because she used to be a nurse, but sometimes witnesses on Sky News said, 'I can't believe it – she was just an ordinary woman who lived next door.'

Jean doesn't live anywhere. People don't like the homeless; they say they stink and should get a job.

'I'd like to see half of them get a job if they were

starving hungry and freezing cold,' Jean had said, when I'd told her.

Jean used to have a big house in Wollaton with her husband and her son Tim, who wanted to be a pilot. When Tim was killed in a motorbike accident, Jean started to drink so it wouldn't hurt as much. Her husband left her and Jean lost her job.

'I had a mental breakdown,' she said, when we were sitting together on the embankment one day. 'When I got better, I had no husband, no job and no house.'

That's how Jean ended up homeless. It doesn't mean she killed her friend.

The next day, I told Miss Crane all about the homeless man's murder.

'He might have just fallen into the water,' Miss Crane said. 'You mustn't jump to conclusions.'

Falling into the water sounded boring. I felt sure Martin Brunt could find the killer.

I wrote him a letter in class.

Dear Martin Brunt,
There has been a ~~death~~ murder
of a homeless person in our river.
The man was Jean's friend. Can you
come with your cameraman and
bring the Criminology experts?

11

After I've worked at the Evening
Post for a bit, I want to work with
you at Sky News.
Yours sincerely,
Kieran Woods
Class 9
c/o Meadows Comprehensive School,
Nottingham

Miss Crane was pleased I'd remembered that it's 'Yours sincerely' when you know someone's name and 'Yours faithfully' when you don't. Before I put the letter in an envelope, I crossed out 'death' and wrote 'murder'.

Miss Crane didn't see me do it.

3

EVIDENCE

When I got in from school Mum still wasn't home, so I went straight to my room and read through my notes again to make sure that I hadn't missed any important pieces of evidence. Then I got my sketchbook out.

I keep this hidden under the bed next to my notebook. It contains pictures I've drawn of stuff that some people might not want others to see.

'Sensitive information', Miss Crane calls it.

You can show sensitive information very well in pictures, if you are good at drawing. You don't need words.

I'm the best at drawing in my class and the best in the whole school. I'm not even being big-headed. I can look at something once or twice, then draw it with my pencils so it looks like a photograph.

It's easy-peasy.

I like my drawing pencils. I keep them in a special wooden box. There are twelve pencils but the matching sharpener is missing. The gold lettering on the box lid says: *Graphite Pencil Sketching Set 5B–5H*. I won them last year at school in a competition called 'Best Young Artist'.

All the schools in Nottingham were in the competition.

Only the people who were good at drawing got to send a picture in.

The writer Julia Donaldson judged it. She works with an illustrator who draws awesome pictures so she knows what good drawings look like.

I won the bit of the competition for people my age and a bit older.

'The under-sixteens category,' said Miss Crane.

There was a prize ceremony for the winners at the Council House. Mum said she'd try and get there but her and Tony had had a row and she didn't want everyone to see her eye. When I went up on stage to get my certificate and pencil box, everyone clapped like they knew me. I pretended Mum was there and waved.

Afterwards, while the others were standing with their parents, Miss Crane stayed with me. We had a glass of pretend champagne and little bits of puffy pastry with this tasty filling in. It was brilliant.

When I got home after the ceremony, nobody was in. I sat at the kitchen table waiting for Mum, looking at my drawing and pencil box prize. I felt warm and calm inside. Then the back door opened and before I could hide my stuff, Ryan came in.

'Let's see,' he said, and grabbed my picture. After a minute he asked, 'Could you teach me to draw?' His voice was small. I looked at him but he wasn't grinning – he was serious.

The back door opened again and Tony stomped into the kitchen. He stopped dead in front of us.

Ryan looked at his feet. 'I was just—'

'Just what?'

'Just telling him to get his stupid stuff off the table,' Ryan said, and he swept my drawing and pencil box on to the floor.

I scrabbled to grab my stuff before Ryan could destroy it. The pencils were rolling everywhere but I managed to get them all.

When I got upstairs, I realized that the sharpener was missing. Mum helped me look for it when she got home and she even asked Tony and Ryan if they had seen it but they both said no. It was just gone.

My drawing pencils all look the same but they all have different sorts of lead to draw with. You use the really hard pencil leads for tiny detailed drawing, like eyes. The softer ones are good for filling in, like if you're drawing the sky. The other thing that is really important when sketching is how much you push the pencil down on to your paper. Different pressures make for different shades on your drawing. It's all very complex if you don't know what you're doing.

My favourite artist is a man called Laurence Stephen Lowry. People shortened it to L. S. Lowry. He was an even better drawer than me. Grandma was going to take me to see some of his real-life pictures at a gallery in

Manchester. It was before she fell out with Mum and Tony.

People think Lowry just painted matchstick men and matchstick cats and dogs. There was even a song about it. But he didn't. He painted all sorts of things and did fantastic sketches.

When I won the Best Young Artist competition, Miss Crane bought me a massive book called *L. S. Lowry: The Art and the Artist*, by T. G. Rosenthal. T. G. Rosenthal knows even more about Lowry than I do.

When Lowry's mum died, he got very sad. He stopped painting people and dogs. He painted the sea but didn't put any boats on the water. He painted houses that nobody lived in. They were falling to bits and sinking down into the ground.

When I look at Lowry's *An Island*, it makes my tummy go all funny. In it is a big, old house that used to be grand, standing alone on a little island surrounded by water. Even though it is a house and not a person, it still looks sad and lost.

When I look at this painting, it feels like something is pressing down on my chest. I go all quiet inside, like when I'm curling up under my blanket, away from everyone.

That's what Lowry can do to you without saying a single word.

I picked out a pencil and started to draw all the scenes of evidence from down at the river, like a comic strip, filling the page with little boxes. I drew Jean like one of Lowry's matchstick characters. She got to be in every box.

Ryan's video game was booming downstairs. I could tell if he had shot someone or detonated a bomb by the different noises. While I was drawing, I thought about Mrs Cartwright next door. She has ulcerated legs so can't get upstairs. She even sleeps in her living room, which is joined on to ours, so she can never escape Ryan's noise.

I wanted to draw some pictures of Tony and Ryan in the living room. Ryan would be playing on his game and Tony would be half asleep. Neither of them would see the pack of wild dogs sneaking in at the door. There would be Japanese Akitas, pit bulls and Dobermanns. The dogs would pounce on them both at the same time.

No one would be able to hear Tony and Ryan screaming because of the loud noise of the Xbox. Not even Mrs Cartwright.

The dogs would rip them both to shreds and eat them. Later, when the dogs were gone, I would sneak downstairs and clean up. When Mum came home, she'd be glad it was just me and her again, with no one to upset her. She wouldn't even be bothered they'd both been eaten.

I saved the pictures in my head to draw another day, and concentrated on the murder instead.

I drew from when I first got down to the river and saw Jean crying on the bench, to the divers getting the body out of the water. It took up two full pages of my sketchpad.

When I was finished, I had very detailed notes and drawings.

I had remembered all the little bits of evidence. I packed matchstick people into the scenes, but I kept the background white like Lowry mostly did and just drew the river and close-ups of where the murder took place. This would make any clues much easier to spot.

Martin Brunt was going to be very pleased.

$$\left(4\right)$$

THE VISITOR

The gunfire sounds from downstairs cut off suddenly. That's how I knew Tony had a visitor.

I went to my bedroom door and opened it a tiny bit. I heard Tony coughing and spluttering. I heard the kitchen door shut behind him.

I used to be allowed downstairs. Now people have started visiting, Tony says I have to stay in my room.

My window overlooks the road, so I can still see everything. Sometimes, I sit with my notebook at the window and write stuff down. It feels like I'm in charge of the street.

There was a red Ford Focus outside the house. The passenger window was down and I could see a man's hand and arm flapping about to music that was booming out.

I got out my binoculars that Grandma gave me, from right at the back of my wardrobe. I hide anything I have that's good, so Ryan can't steal it.

You should never look at the sun with binoculars or you could go blind.

My binoculars are very good ones. I know this because the magnification is 10 x 50. The '10' bit means that whatever you are looking at will appear ten times larger than with your own eyes. The '50' bit means the wide distance across, on the lenses.

'The diameter', Miss Crane calls it.

When the diameter of the lenses is bigger, you get more light into your eyes and you can see stuff better. We learned this in science.

The binoculars used to belong to my great-granddad, who I never met. It's hard to think of Grandma being a little girl and having a dad. Grandma told me he fought in the trenches in World War One. She said he got his binoculars long after that, but in my head I like to think he had them in the trenches to spy on the Germans.

When I saw the man's hand ten times bigger through my binoculars, I spotted that his fingertips were all yellow and his nails were bitten. I wrote this down in my notebook and put an equals sign, like this:

smoker = nervous type

Sherlock Holmes always looked at the tiny clues that most people missed. These can tell you important things about someone. Holmes is old-fashioned now but people still love him.

When you notice little things about people, it is called 'the skill of observation'. Not everyone is good at it.

I heard the back door slam and a man walked down the

path. He had a grey hoodie and sweatpants on. The hood was pulled up and he looked left and right as he walked, then back down at the pavement.

He jumped in the car and zoomed off. I had to keep saying the number plate in my head until I had it written down because I only got one look at it.

It had nothing to do with the murder at the embankment but it made me feel good to record the information. I pretended I was on a special mission and it was my job. Tony might make me stay in my room but I am in charge up here. I can sit at the window and do my observation work and he can't say anything.

I heard someone coming upstairs so I jumped on to my bed and hid my notebook, my sketchbook and my binoculars under the pillow. Then I lay down on top of my covers and looked at the ceiling.

There was a big bang as Ryan kicked my door open. It hit the side of my headboard and bounced back again. Ryan came in and stood in front of me pretending he was shooting me with a big machine gun. He made noises like on his game.

Noises can't hurt me. Noises can't hurt me.

I moved my lips but didn't say the words out loud.

'Yo, retard! Wassup?'

I didn't answer him. I carried on looking at the ceiling.

Ryan kicked the side of my bed with his foot. He swept his hand across my bookcase and knocked everything off.

There was a bit of juice left in a glass and it spilt on my school trousers.

I stayed still. I didn't even blink.

Ryan laughed and went into the bathroom, leaving my door wide open.

I wondered what time Mum would be back. Ryan usually leaves me alone when she's around, but if Mum was on a late shift she could be out for hours more.

I grabbed my sweatshirt and ran downstairs and out of the house before Ryan came back out of the bathroom. It was past teatime, so the light had started to fall out of the sky.

I breathed the fresh air into my lungs but didn't take a really deep breath. The air wasn't properly fresh until you got close to the river. There are no cars down there.

I walked to the bottom of our road and turned on to Court Street. Mrs Denman was trimming her front hedge. The houses either side had messy gardens, one even had an old settee in it, but Mrs Denman always kept hers neat.

When you get to the end of Court Street, it feels like the world opens out. There are trees and grass and the river. The trees are nearly all still in leaf, even though it's October.

Everyone round here calls it the 'embankment'. In summer, girls sit on the grass next to the water, with short skirts and crop tops on. If you walk by slowly, you can sometimes see their knickers but you're not supposed to do this.

When my class took their SATs exams in the summer, I had to do a project. It wasn't sent away to be marked like everyone else's work but it was still important.

Miss Crane said I should choose something I was really interested in to write about, but not Robin Hood because I always did stuff about him.

She made me an A4 booklet. I wrote 'The River Trent by Kieran Woods' on the front. I went on the computer in the school library at dinner-times and found out loads of stuff, which I kept in the working bit of my brain and out of my subconscious.

On the first page of my project book, I wrote all the facts I knew about the river.

- It is 171 miles long.
- It is a BORE river which means it is tidal, like the sea.
- The beginning of the river is called the SOURCE.
- The end of the river is called the MOUTH.
- Part of it flows NORTH, which is unusual for a river.
- People take drugs under the bridge, near the embankment where they think nobody can see them.

- The council men put on protective suits and collect the used syringes once a month so nobody catches AIDS.

Miss Crane went mad about it. She said I'd done brilliantly, but to take the last two facts off because, even though they were true, they were about people and not the river itself. So I did, as it wasn't really fair on the Trent.

When Tony or Ryan get in a bad mood for no reason, I go to the embankment. If it's raining, I can stand just under the bridge, as the druggies don't come until night-time.

The ducks, coots, moorhens, swans and geese don't care if it's raining – they're not like people.

Coots are my favourite. They're awesome. For starters, they're nearly all black apart from a pure white teardrop on their forehead. The second thing is, they dive down deep into the river to catch food and they can stay there for ages. You just start to think they must have drowned when they pop back up again. They are brilliant.

I like it that the river always tries to find its way back to the sea. It never gets tired or gives up; it just does it without even thinking.

5

MAGGOTS AND SHARKS

There were people everywhere on the embankment, scurrying about like Lowry's matchstick figures and talking to each other. Maybe some of them were trying to find out what had happened to the homeless man yesterday.

I stood and watched from the pavement across the road. I knew all the details about the body in the river and I liked knowing that I could help them if I wanted to.

I had written down everything in my notebook and drawn lots of pictures in my sketchbook. All the evidence was safe under my pillow.

Jean was not on her bench. Two older boys from school were slumped on it, smoking.

An old lady walked by. She was holding the hand of a little boy. They weren't looking at the river, or standing at the edge of the embankment where Jean's friend was murdered. They were talking to each other.

My grandma lives in Mansfield. It's about ten miles away. She used to come to Nottingham on the train once a fortnight and stay over for the night. She slept in my bed and I had a sleeping bag on the floor.

It felt like she belonged to me because she stayed

in my room. Sometimes, Grandma would light a little candle and we'd have a midnight picnic with crisps and juice, even though it wasn't really midnight.

That was how me and Grandma used to be.

At first, when I got down the embankment, I'd felt proud I knew all the details of the murder. Now I'd started thinking about Grandma, it felt like my heart had a crack on it. Once your heart is cracked, it can't be mended. It can never be all smooth, like before.

I won't die or anything just because I don't see Grandma any more. Sometimes, when I look at myself in the bathroom mirror, I look like Lowry's *Manchester Man*. His eyes are red and his face is sort of crumpling in on itself. My nose and mouth and ears are all there and look the same. But you can see my cracked heart when you look into my eyes. When this happens, you have to think about your favourite *CSI* episode or do a drawing to take your mind off it.

You can see people all around with cracked hearts. People just walk by one another in the street or in Poundland. They don't look at each other, but if you use the skill of observation you can see that some people's eyes look sad. If something happens to crack your heart, it makes your eyes go dull.

I couldn't understand why all the police had gone. They should still have been investigating. It can take months to solve a murder. There wasn't even any yellow tape with *Police Line Do Not Cross* written on it.

I crossed over the road to get a bit closer. Someone had put some flowers on the edge of the riverbank. If you put flowers at a place where someone died, it means you want to remember them and say you are sorry they died.

'To show respect,' Miss Crane had explained, when I'd asked her about some flowers tied to a lamp post near school.

People had tried to show respect to Jean's friend but they hadn't put them in the right place. They needed to be nearer to the bridge.

I walked over to the flowers and picked up both bunches. I started to walk down towards the bridge to put them in the proper spot.

'Oi!' Someone shouted. 'He's nicking 'em!'

I turned round and the boys from school were pointing at me. Some adults came over.

'Haven't you got any respect for the dead?' a woman demanded.

'They're in the wrong place,' I said. 'Jean's friend was further down there.'

'He was just a homeless tramp,' the boy from school said.

'He still wanted his life,' I said. 'He didn't want to die.'

The woman took the flowers off me.

'I'm putting these back,' she said. 'Don't let me catch you with them again.'

I walked down a bit and stood in the proper place the man died. It was still a grave, even though it was made of water. There was no headstone and no flowers, but the man had died there and that's what counted.

I closed my eyes.

Our Father, who art in heaven. Hallowed be Thy name. Thy kingdom come, Thy will . . .

Something hard hit me on my shoulder. I could hear people laughing but I didn't turn round. Thud. This time on the back of my head. Someone was throwing oranges, hard.

I said I was sorry to Jean's friend in my head, then turned my back on the river.

It was the older boys from school. There were three of them now. One held the bag of oranges behind his back but I could still see them.

'I saw the dead body,' I said.

'Yeah, right,' one said.

'You liar,' said another.

'Prove it,' said the boy with ginger hair.

'His body was bloated three times its normal size,' I said. 'The police pulled it out on to the riverbank and laid him out on a plastic sheet.'

They didn't say anything. I took a few steps towards them.

'He'd been swimming and got pulled under by the current,' I said. 'He had maggots coming out of his eyes.'

One of the boys looked pale.

'His intestines were hanging out. Sharks had eaten half his insides.'

'Sharks? Not in the Trent, you bleeping spaz!'

They laughed and started throwing oranges again.

I carried on down to the bridge, like I wasn't bothered. When the oranges had gone, they walked off, laughing.

Down near the bridge, it was quiet. There were no druggies. I stood in front of the statue of Sir Robert Clifton and looked up at him. His eyes looked a bit sad, like his heart might have been cracked too.

We learned at school he was a politician. He tried to make things better for the working people. At first he was pelted with rocks. Then he became a hero.

He died of typhoid in the end. Typhoid makes rose-coloured spots come on your chest and your nose starts bleeding. When you get a fever and diarrhoea, you are nearly dead. We don't get it in Great Britain any more but people in Africa still die from it.

Jean's friend didn't get typhoid but he was still killed. There are a million and one ways to die in this life.

It's best not to think about it.

6

THINKING IN A DIFFERENT WAY

When I got back home, Mum was in the kitchen making tea.

'Here's my big strong lad,' she said as she chopped up salad. 'Missed seeing you yesterday, love. Did you sort yourself some tea?'

She turned to look at me. Her eyes were bloodshot and her eyelids looked swollen and heavy, as if they were trying to shut out the light.

'There was a murder yesterday down at the embankment,' I said.

She stopped chopping tomatoes and looked at me.

'One of these days your lies are going to get you in hot water,' she said.

'It's true, Mum,' I said. 'I saw the body.'

She shook her head and went back to chopping.

I stood at the lounge door. Ryan wasn't in the room and his game was on pause. Tony was lying on the couch.

'There was a murder yesterday down at the embankment,' I said again.

'Course there was,' said Tony, without opening his eyes. 'There'll be another one in here in a minute, if tha' don't get lost.'

I listened at the bottom of the stairs. Ryan and his spotty friend Reece came charging down, their arms full of Xbox games. They didn't say anything as they pushed past but Reece threw a game case at me. It hit the side of my arm.

You spotty bleep, I said in my head. It's not as bad as saying it out loud and, anyway, he deserved it.

I ran upstairs and shut my bedroom door.

I pulled out my sketchpad and drew the people I'd just seen down at the river, even though there wasn't much evidence. It made the panicky feeling go away.

When I'd drawn the picture, I went back downstairs, into the kitchen.

'What's Grandma's address?' I asked Mum.

She looked at the doorway.

'Just leave it,' she said in her quiet voice.

'I miss her,' I said.

She started to look mad but then her face went soft again.

'Me too,' she whispered. Her eyes were all shiny.

She turned round to the cooker as if she was busy but she wasn't really doing anything. She was trying to stop her eyes being so shiny that tears would fall out and never stop.

We had shepherd's pie for tea. It was delish. You can say just half of some words and people still know what you mean.

My French teacher, Miss Boucher, is very pleased with the way I say the foreign words.

'Pronunciation', Miss Crane calls it.

French people only pronounce half of nearly every single word. If you don't know how to say a French word properly, you just have to leave the end letters off and you get it right.

Miss Boucher wrote 'petit chat' on the whiteboard. It means 'little cat'. You had to put your hand up in class if you thought you knew how to say it. Liam Thornton said 'petit chat' exactly like that with all the letters in it. He got it wrong. Other people put their hands up, but I didn't.

'Kieran,' said Miss Boucher. 'Why don't you have a go?'

I crossed off the last letter of each word in my mind.

'Peti cha,' I said. Miss Crane didn't even help me.

Now people think I'm good at French, but I prefer English because you don't have to waste any letters. I can't understand why French people write the extra letters at the end, if they're not going to say them.

You can be good at anything you want, like pronouncing words or other stuff that's supposed to be hard. All you have to do is find a way. It's like a secret. But it works.

Sometimes, I try and make my mind work in a different way to how it wants to. Then I feel like I'm getting closer to solving how to do something.

Albert Einstein was good at thinking in a different way. It helped him discover a really important scientific thing about light.

'The theory of relativity,' said Miss Crane when we looked at it in class.

He didn't get the answers the way that normal scientists do. They sit down and work out really hard sums and stuff, until they understand an idea. What Albert did was imagine he was riding by the side of a light beam, which is mint. It helped him understand about how fast light travels and stuff, and he found out the answer. He did it by thinking in a different way.

I didn't know Grandma's address. The normal way of thinking told me to ask my mum, who wouldn't tell me.

When I went back upstairs to my room, I closed my eyes and imagined I was Albert Einstein. It felt funny thinking that I had a grey moustache and crazy, wild hair. Albert didn't care what he looked like – he was only bothered about his brain.

I imagined walking by the side of Grandma. I remembered how her tweed coat felt when I touched it. In my mind, I looked up at her brightly patterned headscarf that she always wore when we went shopping. I heard our feet walking on the pavement. I tasted the blackcurrant cream tarts that Grandma always bought from Gents bakers. The cream was piped around the edge so you could still see the blackcurrants through the little circle gap left in the middle.

Grandma had false teeth. When she was in the house, she took them out. I liked her face best without them; it looked more like the real her. When we went out, even just down to the corner shop, she put her teeth in and she looked stricter, even though she was just the same with me.

I opened my eyes and blinked them to get rid of the pictures in my head. I was supposed to be thinking like Albert Einstein, not Kieran Woods.

When I closed my eyes again, I remembered that when I was at primary school my asthma was really bad. It would come on in the yard at break sometimes and I'd feel really unwell, even after using my inhaler. The ladies in the office would ring for my mum to come and get me. If she didn't answer the phone, Grandma came. Even if she had to get a taxi and it cost loads, she didn't care because she wanted me to be safe.

The school didn't have to ask my mum for Grandma's address – they already had it on their computer.

'Thank you, Albert Einstein,' I said out loud in my bedroom.

He had helped me to figure out a different way.

7

SIMILES AND METAPHORS

On the weekends, Mum doesn't have to go to her cleaning job but she still works at the Spar shop on the till until late.

We sat together at the kitchen table after breakfast and went through my English Language book. Ryan wasn't up and Tony was watching sport.

I showed her my work on nouns, verbs and adjectives. I saw her hide a yawn behind her hand.

'I was reading in the *Evening Post* about the body in the river,' she said.

'He was Jean's friend,' I said. 'It looked like rags in the water but his head was in the middle.'

'I've told you not to go near that old tramp woman,' Mum said. 'You'll catch fleas, or worse.'

'Jean hasn't got many friends.'

'I'm not surprised. What happened?'

'He was murdered. The police are trying to find the man. They want me to help them like on *CSI*, because I was first on the scene.'

Mum sighed and looked at the clock. I was worried she was going to say, 'That's it for today,' which always means the end of our time together.

She turned the pages of the workbook, looking at my pencilled answers.

'I don't know how you remember the difference between a simile and a metaphor,' she said, ruffling my hair.

It's great when me and Mum can sit on our own for a bit. It's like it used to be.

'A simile is when you say something is *like* something else,' I said. 'Kieran's mum is LIKE a beautiful rose. That's a simile.'

Mum laughed.

'You charmer,' she said.

'A metaphor is when you say something actually *is* something else. Like saying Tony IS a lazy pig.'

I laughed and looked up at Mum. But her face was all drooping down. She looked like she was going to be sick.

I hadn't heard Tony come into the kitchen.

Tony hit me hard on the side of my head. I fell off my chair and banged the back of my head.

'No!' screamed Mum. 'Leave him alone!'

Tony stood over me. His face was red, like a beetroot. That is a simile.

'You little bleep,' he said.

Tony normally shouts but instead he was talking quietly, through his teeth. It meant he was really, really mad.

'Don't hit him,' said Mum, twisting her hands.

'I'll do what the hell I like. Don't tell me what to do in my own home, woman.'

I sat up and rubbed my sore head.

'It was a metaphor,' I explained.

'Don't push me,' said Tony, kicking the chair.

Ryan came to the doorway.

'Can't he go in a retards' home or something?' he asked.

'This is my home,' I said.

Tony crouched down right next to me. He came into the private space that Miss Crane taught me you have to respect with other people. She said it was very important and it's OK to tell people if you feel uncomfortable.

'This is MY home, daft lad. Mine. So don't you forget it.' He looked up at Mum and then back to me. 'I say who lives here, so watch your bleeping mouth.'

I could smell his sweaty skin. When he spoke, his breath touched my cheek.

'You're too close,' I said, looking at the floor. 'This is my private space.'

Tony knocked me sideways and I hit my forehead on the cooker.

'No!' screamed Mum, and rushed forward to pull Tony away.

'Stay out of it,' he snarled.

My mum was crying. I was crying. I buried my head between my knees. When you're scared, it's hard to know how to do the right thing.

Ryan came up to me and kicked me hard on both shins. I didn't make a sound.

I closed my eyes and pretended I was riding away on a beam of light.

When Tony and Ryan had gone back into the living room, Mum helped me up and bathed the cut on my head.

'Are you OK?' Her voice was hoarse, like when she's done karaoke at the pub.

I said I was all right, but really I felt a bit sick and dizzy.

When Mum went to work, she said I should go down to the embankment. She said it was best for me to stay out of their way until she got home.

It was drizzly rain, so I put my anorak on. Me and Mum walked down the road together until she had to turn off for the Spar.

We didn't talk much. Mum didn't even put her umbrella up. The rain made all the curls fall out of her hair. It looked darker, now it was wet. I told her it reminded me of the gerbils' tails at school.

She said nothing. It was as if she couldn't hear me.

She wouldn't laugh, or anything. Even when I told her a Doctor, Doctor joke.

She just did her lips in a little tight, straight line and she usually loves it.

I tried another one.

'Doctor, Doctor—'

'Kieran,' said Mum. 'Just leave it.'

It's tricky to know the difference between when to make people laugh and when to stay quiet.

I kissed Mum on the cheek before she turned left on to Queen's Walk.

The embankment was quiet. All the people from yesterday were in their houses with the heating on, watching the telly and eating snacks.

I walked down to the river. The flowers were still in the wrong place. I looked around to check nobody was watching. Then I picked them up and took them a bit further down towards the bridge, to the real water grave.

When I looked up from the water, I saw two people coming.

It was the police.

8

AUTOPSY

'How's our young sleuth?'

The policeman grinned, like he'd told a good joke.

'When are the divers coming back?' I said.

The policewoman said, 'They're not coming back, love. They've finished their work here now.'

They both had name badges on. The man's said *PC Sandeep Malik*, and the woman's said *PC Emma Bennett*.

'Hasn't a young lad like you got anything better to do than be hanging around here, in the rain?' asked PC Malik.

'You forgot to put the police tape up,' I said. 'There might still be clues here about the killer.'

PC Bennett sighed. 'Let's not get carried away. He probably just fell in.'

'He was old,' I said. 'He could have been pushed in.'

PC Malik looked annoyed. 'Speculation is a dangerous thing, young man,' he said. 'There's no evidence to suggest that. We'll see what the post-mortem results say.'

'Post-mortem' means 'after death'. In America, they say 'autopsy' instead.

A special doctor called a pathologist carries out the

post-mortem, to find clues about how a person died. They do a Y-incision on your chest so they can take your organs out and weigh them. They even have to take your brain out, which is gross.

If they think someone died suspiciously, the coroner has to make a decision about what happened. They write the reason on the death certificate.

I learned it from watching *CSI*. I told a Year Seven boy all about it at break one day. I did it so he knew what would happen to his granddad, who had just died.

After that, Miss Crane said she wanted a 'quick word'. They say that at school when you are going to get told off.

She explained that people get upset about that sort of thing, especially when a loved one has died, and that I should stop dwelling on it.

'It's morbid,' she said.

Jean came out from under the bridge. She waved to me and started shuffling towards us with all her blankets and bin bags in the old shopping trolley.

'Not that daft old bat again,' muttered PC Bennett.

When she got near us, Jean said, 'If he'd been a copper, would you be doing more?'

'We haven't got time for this,' said PC Malik. 'Have a nice day, you two.'

'They don't give a toss,' Jean said, when they'd gone. 'Colin was just a useless old tramp in their eyes.'

She looked at the flowers on the concrete and a tear slid from her eye. I watched it run down her cheek and into the deep wrinkled crease that went from the corner of her mouth, right down to her chin.

'Colin Kirk, bless his soul,' she said. 'He was kind to me. Even gave me one of his blankets last winter, when we couldn't get a bed in the hostel.'

'If it was just me and my mum, you could come and live with us, Jean.'

She smiled but she still looked sad. She reached over and touched the cut on my forehead.

'I did it on the cooker,' I said.

'Like your mammy. She's always banging into things, isn't she?'

I looked down at my feet. There were little pebbles there, all shapes and sizes. I wondered how they got there, where they were from.

'There used to be a big chain ferry here before the bridge was built. It took food and people and animals over the river,' I said. 'It was in the seventeenth century.'

'Did there, lad?' Her voice was soft.

A line of ducks swam past us. Three boys with coloured feathers and a girl with brown feathers. They didn't even look our way.

'I wish the ducks could speak,' I said. 'They see everything that goes off on the river.'

'And the Canada geese,' said Jean. 'They gabble on all

the time. They'd have a story or two to tell us if we could understand them, eh, Kieran?'

If someone asks you something but it doesn't need an answer, it's called a 'rhetorical question'. Jean asked a lot of rhetorical questions. I didn't mind because she was my friend.

You can tell a lot from a person's body language, before they even say anything. Some police experts in America can even tell if someone is guilty or not, by seeing which way their eyes look when they're being questioned.

'If I was twenty years younger, I'd find out what happened myself,' said Jean, looking down into the water. 'If it's left to the police, someone is going to get away with murdering poor Colin.'

And that's what gave me the idea.

9

ONE OF THE FAMILY

On Sunday, Mum told me to stay out of Tony's way before she went to work. It was too rainy to go out, so I stayed in my room all day thinking about Grandma and about Colin's murder. By the time I went to bed my brain was so full of scheming that it was even trying to plan during the night and woke me up. I actually wished it was morning but my clock said *4:40* and that is too early for breakfast.

I'd already got my underpants on when Mum tapped on my door in the morning, so I put on my socks and school shirt.

Mum says it's important to keep clean but I don't have a shower every day. For one thing, hardly any water comes out of the shower head. It stops sometimes, then a big bit of water comes out and nearly drowns you. Another thing is, it is freezing cold because the immersion heater never gets put on. Money doesn't grow on trees.

When Mum came into my room, I was nearly dressed.

'Kieran's an early bird this morning,' she said, and sat down next to me on the bed.

Normally, I like it when she talks like that, but this

44

morning I didn't like it because she had a big bruise on her jaw and another on her arm. There were red marks on her neck.

Sometimes, if you pretend you don't notice things, you can forget about them. It's like you never saw them in the first place. I couldn't do that because the bruises were too big.

'He hurt you again,' I said.

The words cracked in my throat and came out higher than my normal voice.

'I'm fine,' she said in her happy voice, but it didn't sound real. 'How about scrambled eggs for breakfast?'

Scrambled eggs with grated cheese on top is my favourite breakfast of all time.

'I'm not hungry.'

Mum rubbed the back of my head, where the lump was.

'Grandma tried to stop him hurting you,' I said.

Mum put her head in her hands.

'Kieran, will you please stop mentioning Grandma,' she said.

'I want to see her,' I said. 'Tony hurts you, but you still do as he says.'

The words sounded strange, like I was the boss.

'It's my own fault,' Mum said. When she moved her hands away, tears were there. 'I wind him up. I should learn to keep my mouth shut.'

My guts felt like when I needed a poo, except I didn't want one.

If it was just me and Mum, I could look after her better. When I'm grown up, the fat will turn into hard, bulging muscles like on the *World's Strongest Man*. Then nobody will hurt my mum.

'Grandma said he's nothing but a bully,' I said quietly in Mum's ear.

Grandma also said Tony was a violent, stinking pig who needed castrating, but I didn't say that in case he was near the door again. Grandma didn't care. She said it in front of Tony's face. She is the bravest grandma ever.

'He's been good to us, Kieran. He took us into his home.'

Mum put her arm round me and held me tight. It felt like a metal band across my shoulders. It felt like I couldn't move and Tony was winning.

I stood up and her arm fell away.

'I have to put my school trousers on,' I said.

Mum's face went all crumply and she looked really sad. Miss Crane's face looked like that when Rex, her dog, died last Christmas. She said she loved Rex like he was one of the family. It was hard to know how she felt.

'Sometimes, it helps to put yourself in the place of the other person,' Miss Crane said. 'It helps you to understand, Kieran.'

I put myself in Miss Crane's place. I imagined that Rex

was my dog. Then, I thought about Tony's dog, Tyson. He's not like one of the family. When we moved in, Tyson bit Mum. Tony said he was only playing but after he bit Ryan too, he had to go and live in the shed, at the top of the garden.

I looked at the matchstick dogs in my Lowry book. He painted them running and jumping or just standing still next to their masters. Lowry loved dogs; he always painted them next to people. They were full of life and never dead. He never shut them up so they were all alone.

I still didn't feel like crying.

I looked at my mum, sitting on my bed. Snot was running down from her nose.

'Want a game of Monopoly?' I said.

She shook her head.

'Snap?'

She smiled a bit but it still meant no.

I sat next to her again and touched the new dark red mark on her temple.

When I put my arms round her, she started to cry.

'I've made such a mess of it all,' she sobbed. 'Dragged you into it and everything.'

She always said stuff like that after Tony had got mad.

'I love you, Mum,' I said. Then I got up quickly and started to pull on my trousers.

She stopped crying and looked up at me.

'Oh, Kieran, I . . .'

She started to cry, harder than before. It's hard to figure girls out.

When I was dressed I sat back down on the bed next to her. I didn't want to hug her again but I put my hand on her shoulder. It meant I cared about her, like Miss Crane cared about her dog. It meant I needed her and she needed me.

I just wish Tony would hurt me every time, instead of her.

⑩

FORENSICS

I got to school ten minutes before the bell.

I stood in my place in the far corner of the playground, under the monkey-puzzle tree. I like it there because I can see everything that's happening but nobody notices me. Sometimes, I pretend the monkey-puzzle tree's branches make me invisible.

I watched all the different-coloured faces, zapping about the playground like short bolts of lightning. I could see the puffs of breath in front of their faces as they shouted and screamed at each other.

I don't like running around willy-nilly. I like to be quiet and still.

While I stood calmly, my brain was working like the inside of a watch. All the cogs were turning, bits were ticking.

My brain told me that the best way to get Grandma's address was from the school office. This is what happens when you start to think like Albert Einstein.

There is a nice lady who works there. Her name is Lisa. The boss lady in the office is called Janet. She has glasses with thin, black frames and her hair is grey, like dry wire. Her face always looks like she's chewing something nasty.

Once, I heard our Science teacher, Mr Jefferson, say that Janet was an old witch. He said it to Miss Crane in a low voice, while I was preparing copper sulphate crystals for an experiment, just after lunch.

It was important for me to ask the right office lady for the information. To increase my chances of success, I had to think about every possible outcome of my actions.

There was this murderer once on a crime programme I used to watch with Grandma. He wanted to commit the perfect crime. He thought about it for a long time before he did it. He tried to think of every possible outcome, just like me and Albert Einstein.

But he left a vital piece of evidence at the scene of the crime because he rushed it at the end. Instead of asking the old janitor to dispose of a bag of rubbish, he asked the cleaner. She was nosy and when he had gone, she went through the bag and found his bloodstained gloves. Big mistake.

The bell rang and everyone went in for registration. When I got to my class, Miss Crane was waiting for me, sitting next to my empty chair, like always.

'That's a nasty cut on your head, Kieran,' she said.

'I fell off my bike.'

She carried on looking at it until I turned my head away.

'You know you can talk to me about anything that's wrong, don't you?' she said. 'I mean, *anything* at all.'

'Yes,' I said. 'But nothing is wrong.'

First lesson was Maths. Boring. Second lesson was Art. Brilliant.

Mrs Bentley brought over my seascape picture and unrolled it on the table. Art tables are the best. It doesn't matter how big your work is, it always fits. It has slots to hold your paper and you can put it at a tilt, so it's easier to get to the far bits. I wished I had one in my bedroom.

We were working with pastels, so I got to wear some thin, rubber disposable gloves like a pathologist.

Pastels have pigment in that can stain your hands. It's hard to wash off. Sometimes it can stay on your hands for ages. If blood was like that, it would be much easier to find killers. The only way you can see blood when it has been cleaned up is by using UV light. 'UV' is short for 'ultra-violet'.

UV light is the best. It can find bloodstains, even if the killer has tried to wash them away or has painted over them. What happens is that the blood absorbs all the light and doesn't reflect it back. So the stains show up as black.

Forensic experts can take samples of the black stains and do scientific tests to prove if they are definitely blood. Then the police can catch the killer. Science is brilliant for finding hidden evidence from crimes.

I was creating a seascape like one of Lowry's. In his *Seascape 1960*, he drew a view of the North Sea from the north-east coast. Lowry just used pencil on paper but Mrs

Bentley said we had to use pastels, which was annoying.

I was using grey and plum pastels for my picture, even though most people make the sea bright blue in paintings. My sea looked massively lonely and miserable.

'Bleak,' said Miss Crane.

It felt like I was drawing the fizzy lump in the middle of my chest but it came out as the sea. The lump pressed against my heart when I thought about Mum's bruises.

'Interesting,' said Mrs Bentley when she got round to my table. 'Are we going to have some birds in that sky?'

'No,' I said.

'Perhaps we could have a little more differentiation between the sea and the sky?'

I liked Mrs Bentley, but not her paintings. They were all over the walls of the art room. She only did butterflies and flowers and they didn't even look real. They were all in bright colours and the sun was always shining. They didn't make me feel like anything inside.

Lowry is a much better Art teacher. All you have to do is look at his paintings and your worries go away. Everything outside the paintings seems small and you just know things are going to be OK. Lowry knew more about drawing and painting than Mrs Bentley ever will, even though she has letters after her name that mean she is an expert.

'It's supposed to be bleak,' I said.

Mrs Bentley raised her eyebrows at Miss Crane and

they did a secret smile at each other.

At the end of the class, Miss Crane helped me roll my seascape back up. Next lesson it would be finished.

'You can take it home with you then, to show your mum,' she said.

I pretended I hadn't heard her.

After break, it was time for PE. I hate PE the most out of every subject we do at school. This is why:

1. PE teachers only like you if you're good at sport.
2. Miss Crane doesn't stay with me in PE – I have to do it on my own.

We did indoor football in the big gym because it was raining.

Craig Durham and Matthew Pounder are the best at sport. They are Mr Strachan's favourites and they always get to choose their teams.

At the end of the choosing, there was just me and Thomas Brewer left. Thomas is so fat his trousers get holes in them where his wobbly thighs rub together. His mum buys him new ones but it always happens again.

It makes everybody in the class laugh. Apart from Thomas.

11

THE OLD WITCH

At lunchtime, I limped over to the school office.

I hadn't really hurt my ankle but if you want people to believe something it's important to act like it is true.

When I got to the hatch, there were two other people there waiting. The girl at the front was paying some dinner money in. I felt sick when the office lady came back with her change. It was the wire-haired boss woman, Janet.

My heart started to beat so hard I could feel it in my head and even in the ends of my fingers. I did a silent prayer that the sea noise wouldn't start, because I can't hear anything else when it does.

The girl went away and the boy in front of me got served. He needed the register for Class 7R, which made her tut.

When I got to the front, the boss lady looked about seven feet tall, which is as tall as an American basketball player. Her glasses magnified her eyes nearly as well as my great-granddad's binoculars.

'For the second time, YES?'

The sea sound started. It whooshed in my ears, making me dizzy. I held on to the shelf at the hatch. I could see her wrinkly mouth moving but I couldn't hear any of the words.

I think I said, 'I feel sick.'

The office door opened and the other lady, Lisa, came out. She sat me down on one of the soft padded chairs in reception and waited quietly, until the sea sound went away.

'Do you feel OK, Kieran?'

I nodded.

'The old witch made the sea sound come in my head,' I said.

Lisa's face looked funny, like she was holding her breath against hiccups. Her lips actually seemed glued together.

She breathed and let her lips go. Then she smiled with teeth.

'What is it you wanted, love?'

My heart was drumming again. *Boom, boom, boom.* Telling lies is bad.

'I hurt my ankle in PE,' I said. 'Miss Crane sent me to get Grandma's telephone number and address.'

Lisa frowned. 'We usually ring from the office,' she said. 'Is your mum at work?'

It was all going wrong.

'Mum is at work,' I said. 'Miss Crane said she needs to speak to my grandma about something else.'

Lisa looked at me. I kept my eyes looking straight

ahead and tried not to blink. If you are a body language expert and someone looks to the right, it means they are making stuff up that hasn't happened yet. If they blink too much, or scratch their ears or nose, it definitely means they are telling lies.

'We're not supposed to give any personal information out from the office,' she said. 'It's to do with data protection. Miss Crane knows that.'

It wasn't going to work.

'I know Grandma's number but it's locked up inside my subconscious,' I said.

Lisa smiled.

'I'm sure you do,' she said. 'Wait here.'

She went back into the office.

A long time went by. Maybe she was ringing the staff room to speak to Miss Crane. She might have called the Spar shop and be talking to Mum. She couldn't ring the home phone because Virgin Media had cut the line off until Tony paid the bill.

The old witch came to the window and glared at me. She slammed the hatch glass closed so hard, I thought it was going to break and cut her fingers off.

To get her back, I made up a picture in my head of her screaming with blood all over the hatch glass. All her fingers were cut off; two of them were on the floor in front of me but I didn't pick them up. They still had short, dark-pink nails on them. She was holding up her hand while she screamed and there was only a thumb left on it.

'Kieran? You OK?'

Lisa stood in front of me.

The hatch wasn't broken; there were no fingers on the floor.

'You don't seem well,' she said, and gave me a piece of paper. 'There's your grandma's number, love. Tell Miss Crane to come and see me if she needs the address.'

⑫

A HERO'S STORY

There was a telephone box down the bottom of the estate.

I had a piggy bank in my bedroom. When I got back home, I was going to count the money. I hoped I had enough for a phone call to Grandma.

I walked home from school the long way, past the embankment. It had stopped raining and I could hear the moorhens and geese.

When I got round the corner, I stopped. There was a group of people standing right where I'd found Colin's dead body.

The sky was grey; the water was grey. The people all had dark clothes on. They were standing in a little huddle.

It looked exactly like Lowry's oil painting scene, *The Funeral*, except there was no church or gravestones in the background, just the river. I couldn't see their faces or hear what they were saying, but the sadness dripped off them. It was sadness that Lowry painted, not the people's faces. That's how he made you feel it.

I walked nearer. Stopped. Walked nearer.

I pretended I was looking at the river until I was standing right next to them.

There were two ladies and three men. The ladies were crying and the men looked sad.

'It's just not good enough,' said the man with the bald head. 'They won't tell us *anything*.'

'They said they had nothing much to tell us,' said one of the ladies. 'That he probably just fell in.'

'Did you want something, young man?'

One of the other men had seen me listening and staring.

Miss Crane has told me before that people don't like it when you stare at them.

'No,' I said.

'Do you live around here?'

His voice sounded posh.

'I live on Maple Street,' I said. 'With my mum and Tony and Ryan.'

'I see,' said the man. He glanced at the others.

'I found Jean's friend dead in the river,' I said.

The lady with the pink scarf let out a squeal and the bald man put his arm round her.

'This is no time for storytelling,' he said. His voice sounded like the teachers at school.

'His name was Colin Kirk,' I said. 'He was a homeless man but he still wanted to live.'

'Oh my God, he's telling the truth,' cried the other lady.

'Can you tell us what happened from the beginning?'

asked the third man. He was quite young but his face looked old and tired.

I told them everything. I told them how Colin's body just looked like rags in the water. I told them the police thought he was drunk and fell in. Then I told them that me and Jean thought he'd been murdered.

The ladies were crying worse than ever. I was worried I'd said something wrong.

'Where might we find this Jean?' the bald man asked.

'She hasn't got a home. Sometimes, she's under the bridge.'

The bald man said something in the lady with the pink scarf's ear and walked off down the embankment.

'Don't look so worried,' the other lady said. 'Thank you for telling us that – it's more than the police have.'

'Did you know Colin?' I said.

'I'm his sister,' she said. 'My name is Deirdre.'

She shook my hand, which I had practised doing with Miss Crane.

'Very pleased to meet you,' I said.

'I'm Colin's cousin,' said the pink-scarf lady. 'And the others are people who knew Colin and cared very much about him.'

'Why couldn't Colin live with you, if you cared about him?'

Deirdre looked at the other lady. She shifted from one foot to the other.

'It's not always that simple,' she said. 'Sometimes people don't want to be helped. They just want to be left alone.'

I hoped Grandma didn't want to be left alone. I hoped she would be glad when I rang her.

I looked down the embankment, towards the bridge. The bald man had disappeared.

When I looked again, he came out from under the bridge. Jean was with him.

When they got to us, Jean walked round the others and came and stood next to me. She smelt like a wet dog.

'This is Jean,' said the man to the others. 'She knew Colin too.'

The others all said hello at the same time. I saw Deirdre looking at Jean's dirty sandals.

Jean didn't say hello back. It meant she wasn't just letting them win.

The lady in the pink scarf said, 'Is this exactly where Colin died?'

Jean and I both looked at the water. We nodded.

'Then this is a good place to tell the story of Colin's remarkable life and the wonderful man he was.' She dabbed at her eyes. 'At least two people round here will know he was more than a homeless pile of rags.'

The bald man coughed and looked at Jean.

'No offence intended,' he said.

'Since Colin was a boy, the only thing he ever wanted

to do was to join the fire brigade. He'd done nearly thirty years' service before a terrible night in Nottingham, when one of the busiest pubs in town suffered an arson attack.'

'He told me he'd been a fireman,' said Jean.

The lady nodded. 'They cleared the pub, got everyone out and took the injured to hospital. Meanwhile, the fire raged worse than ever, despite their efforts to put it out. The landlord had an illegal stash of industrial diesel in the back which had ignited and exploded.'

'Nobody had thought about the flat upstairs,' said the bald man. 'By the time they remembered, the flames had engulfed the stairs. The landlord told the police there was a lady and her three small children in there.'

'They had to send for a longer ladder to reach the flat from the back of the building. Colin realized the family would perish if they waited. So, despite his supervisor forbidding him to enter the burning building, Colin went in.'

'Wicked,' I said.

The lady looked at me with a twisty face. 'He got the lady and two of her children out alive,' she said. 'The baby was already dead. Colin was a hero but he got terribly burned.'

'It took the best part of a year for him to heal and, when he had, the fire brigade told him he was unfit for duty,' said the bald man, looking into the murky depths of the river. 'Saving that family cost Colin his career and his sanity.'

'He went travelling,' continued the lady in the scarf. 'He was looking for something he was never going to find. He was haunted with guilt because he couldn't save the baby.'

'We hadn't heard from him for three years,' Deirdre said. 'The police found my name and address in Colin's bag and contacted me.'

'It's a sad end for a hero,' the young man said.

(13)

BRUISES

Before they left, Deirdre gave Jean a piece of paper with her name and address on. The man gave her some paper money.

I hoped the police wouldn't find it in her bag if she died.

Jean was quiet after they had gone. We both wanted to be on our own.

'I'm going to the hostel,' said Jean. She looked even older than usual.

I wished I could go to the hostel with Jean. I walked over there with her once and sat outside watching.

Loads of homeless people shuffled in through the door. They all looked the same; it didn't matter if they were men or women. They walked the same way. Slowly, like their whole bodies hurt.

Their shoulders stooped like the people in Lowry's crowds. It seemed as if they were all one great big miserable person, they looked so similar.

When you've been living on the streets for a long time, everything about you turns grey and dark, even your lips. Only your eyes stay coloured.

I walked up the far end of the embankment and sat on a bench.

I thought about Colin and how he'd saved the children from the fire. There had been nobody to save Colin from the killer. Now there was nobody to find out what had really happened to him because the police weren't bothered.

I didn't want to go home. I wished Mum was there. I wasn't allowed in the Spar shop when she was working. It was staff rules they couldn't talk to people they knew.

There wasn't anyone else around, even on the other side of the river. I wasn't on my own because there were ducks and coots on the water. You couldn't see them, but under the water were loads of fish, swimming about in their fish families. If you had a magnifying glass, you might even be able to see tiny creatures with one cell, called 'amoebae'.

The ducks and the coots and the fish didn't hurt each other like people do.

Anoraks are good for keeping out the rain but not for staying warm. I started to shiver but I still didn't go home.

I got up from the bench and walked back down to Colin's grave.

If you talk to yourself, people think you're cuckoo. But I wasn't talking to myself – I was talking to Colin's spirit. When you die, you leave your body and become a spirit, like in *Paranormal Activity*. Colin wasn't a scary spirit that haunted people. His spirit just lived in the water now.

'I promise I'll find out what happened, Colin,' I said out loud.

If you say something out loud, it means you are really going to do it. I looked down when I said it. If somebody was secretly watching, they might see my mouth move and think I was cuckoo.

I started to walk back home. I cut up through the estate, on Arkwright Walk.

Arkwright Walk is a big, wide path that goes right through the Meadows. It twists and turns like a river without water. It takes you from one side to the other. It has trees dotted along it and if you make a noise when you're walking on there people in the flats open their windows and scream 'Eff off, you bleep' at you.

It's OK to walk along there when it's light or maybe even dusk. At night all the gangs come out and bring their guns and knives. I've never seen them because kids aren't allowed on here. Carlton Blake said you'd get minced up by blades and they'd put you in a skip where you'd never be found.

As I walked, I looked all around me for clues, like bloodstains on the concrete. If it was dark and I had a UV light, it would be easy. It was going to be hard to find Colin's killer because there wasn't any blood on the ground where he died. Blood is a massive clue that helps the detectives to catch the murderer on nearly every episode of *CSI* I have ever watched.

Halfway down Arkwright Walk I turned left into the estate. I could see the Spar on the corner. There was a bin outside that was full of rubbish that wasn't even from the shop. Someone had propped up an old pushchair without any wheels against it.

The Spar windows were covered in massive food picture stickers, so I had to walk right up close and look in between the gaps.

I saw Mum standing behind the till. She was right next to the window. If I tapped on it, she might wave. Then I remembered the staff rules and what Tony might do if I was to blame for Mum getting sacked.

It would have been perfect if she was at home when I got back, but at least I got to see her through the window. She had put the thick brown stuff on her face to cover up the bruises but you could still see them a bit.

Her polo neck covered up the red marks. Apart from that, she was just like my normal mum.

She was talking to a lady customer. You could tell Mum liked her because she was smiling, showing her teeth. When Mum looked down at the till to get her change, I saw the lady secretly look at the bruise on Mum's jaw.

Mum looked smiley but I could tell that her eyes were still sad. You can easily see it when you know somebody really well. It's harder to do with strangers.

When I got back to our street, I decided to practise my covert-operation techniques. The SAS are always going out on practice jobs where they have to abseil down from helicopters or approach remote farmhouses without being seen. It's the only way to keep sharp until a real emergency situation happens.

I was going to practise my stealth skills on Tony and Ryan.

First, I put my back flat to the wall of the alleyway that runs up the side of the house. I crept along the wall until I was right where the settee is located on the other side. I pretended I had a laser gun that could shoot through walls, but silently, so the police didn't come.

I blasted Tony in the back; then I aimed a bit higher to get Ryan over on the other side of the room, where he sits in his Xbox chair.

Tony bought him the special chair last Christmas. It is made of black leather and has pouches in the arms where you put your Xbox controls. You can even put a mug of tea or a can of beer in a specially made holder in the arm.

I'm strictly not allowed to sit in the chair.

On Christmas morning, Ryan said, 'If I find your stupid ass anywhere near it, I will seriously rip your head off.'

You can't rip someone's head off, not with your bare hands, anyway. There are thick tendons and bones in your neck that hold your head on. Ryan doesn't know anything.

When he kicked the bus shelter glass in and broke his big toe, Tony had to take him to casualty. Mum went upstairs to have a bath and I sat in Ryan's Xbox chair. I could smell the new leather and the back was all cushiony and comfy but I still didn't like it.

Before I got up I did two big farts on it and put a bit of spit off my finger into the bottom of the cup holder. It meant I had won.

I wrote it in my notebook so it was definitely real.

Mum couldn't buy me a big present like Ryan's chair because she had to give Tony all her work money and he didn't give her any back. But it didn't matter because Grandma bought me a great big, hardback book, all about *CSI*.

It tells you all about the series, the forensics and everything. I like every bit of it, except the pages where it gives you the actors' real names and tells you about them in real life. That spoils the book a bit because it's saying that *CSI* isn't about the real LVPD, which stands for 'the Las Vegas Police Department'. It's just pretend.

14

GETTING YOUR OWN BACK

After I had shot Tony and Ryan through the wall, I slipped in through the side gate.

Tyson used to bark when anybody came in the garden but he doesn't bother any more. Tony hardly ever takes him out for a walk since he finished his job at the council. He used to walk around the estate with Tyson every day, but since Tyson bit Ryan and Mum he's lost interest. I think he's scared Tyson will bite him too, which would serve him right.

Mum feeds Tyson when she gets home from work. Sometimes, it's too dark to see up the yard and then he has to wait until the next day. She doesn't really like him because he is a big dog and she is nervous he might bite her again. When she opens the shed door, he gets up but his legs are all stiff. Mum has to hold a tissue to her nose because it stinks in there.

The sitting-room curtains were closed even though it was still light. Ryan always does that so he can see his game better.

I went up the garden and sat down outside Tyson's shed. I heard him moving about inside.

'I wish I could let you out, boy,' I said.

You can call dogs 'boy', even if you're not an adult. It means you like them.

Tyson is big and mean but he whimpered like a little baby behind the door. You are supposed to look after animals. They don't like being on their own all the time or being shut in a small shed without a window. You are not being a good owner if you leave them to sort themselves out.

'It's called "neglect",' Miss Crane said, when I told her at school one day. She hardly ever looks mad, but she did when she heard about Tyson living in the shed.

I do like Tyson, but I don't trust him. You should never trust dogs like him because they can snap at any time and attack you. I heard on the news about a little girl who was brought up with two Rottweilers. They were like babies, normally. The man who owned them said they were 'soft as grease', when he was interviewed on the TV. One day, when her gran was out of the room, the dogs attacked the little girl and she died. The dogs had to be put down, which means they were killed by the vet with an injection.

In America, they have the death penalty, which is awesome but still makes me feel a bit sick. Murderers and other really bad criminals can still be killed by the electric chair, but usually a doctor kills them with a needle. It is called 'Death by Injection'.

Death by Injection is supposed to be a better way to kill someone than electrocuting them until smoke comes out of their ears. But they still die either way, so I don't see the difference.

I left Tyson and sneaked into the kitchen through the back door. Then I stopped still and listened at the hallway door. I imagined I was a policeman, about to do a drugs bust on the house. I could hear the roaring of Ryan's game from the living room. I opened the hallway door a bit and put my head through. When I could see it was all clear, I slipped through and inched along the hall with my back to the wall.

I crept upstairs and shut my bedroom door.

There was a little plastic plug in the belly of my piggy bank. I could hear some money jiggling around inside him. It took me ages to get the plug out. I had to use a pen to get under the top of it.

Monkeys and apes are the most similar animals you can get to a human. I know this because:

a) David Attenborough has filmed them making tools out of sticks to do a job, like reach something in the water or get honey out of a bees' nest.
b) They can touch their first finger with their thumb, which is a very useful thing to be able to do, even though you might not think it is.

An ape or a monkey still couldn't have got the plug out of my piggy bank, though; it was too hard.

When I finally got it out, I stopped and listened for a second. If Ryan burst into my room now he would steal my money and I wouldn't be able to ring Grandma. But I could still hear his game booming through the floor.

I rattled the piggy bank so the coins dropped through the hole. I shook out lots of different coins, all in different amounts.

'Denominations', Miss Crane calls them.

I put the different denominations in my pocket and put the plug back in the pig, only this time a bit looser. Then I hid him behind my KerPlunk game at the back of my wardrobe.

I tucked my notebook and pen inside my anorak and went back downstairs. I peeped through the living-room door. Tony and Ryan were in their usual places. Tony looked like he really had been shot through the back. He had fallen asleep on his side with his mouth wide open.

He looked like he was dead.

The kitchen clock said 5.30 p.m. It would be at least another three hours before Mum got home. She had to go to her cleaning job after working at the Spar shop.

When I got on to the street, I said, 'Tony, you are a lazy stinking pig that wants castrating.' I said it out loud but still a bit quiet . . . just in case.

When I got near the phone box, I could see some lads

in it. I said a prayer that they weren't breaking it so nobody else could use it.

'Vandalism,' Miss Crane had said, when someone ripped my art off the wall at school, 'is a completely senseless crime.'

Older boys from my school liked to do vandalism. I don't know why. If they saw something nice, like flowers in Mrs Denman's garden, they wanted to spoil them so nobody else could enjoy them. They didn't care that Mrs Denman had worked hard to make her garden nicer than the scruffy ones on either side.

If you don't look after your house, it starts to go derelict. Bits fall off and the paint peels away. Houses can look sad, like people. When Lowry felt lonely and sad, he painted abandoned houses and boatyards. When you look at the paintings, you don't just see the lonely places, you feel sad and alone deep in your guts.

Ryan kicked the bus shelter glass in just because he felt like it. A few days later, two council men came and replaced the glass with a special, thick plastic that's much harder to break. They swept up all the broken glass pieces that looked like diamonds on the dirty concrete.

The police didn't attend the scene to try to get fingerprints because all the people who catch the bus would have touched the metal seats, so they wouldn't be able to tell which prints belonged to the perp. You can say 'perp' instead of the full word, 'perpetrator'. It shows you know what you're talking about.

I got my watch out of my jacket pocket. I can't wear it because the plastic strap has snapped.

At 5.50 p.m., the phone vandals left. I waited until they'd turned the corner before I went inside the phone box.

There was half a can of lager on the little shelf and half a bag of crisps. My tummy was grumbly hungry so I ate them, even though they were prawn cocktail flavour and not my favourite, which is cheese and onion.

One of the boys had done a big spit on the phone handle. I could tell it was them because it was still dripping wet with foamy bubbles in it.

I was careful not to touch the spit in case I got a disease. I read the phone instructions three times to get them in order, in my head.

Then I dialled Grandma's number.

15

MISSING PERSON

Brr Brr. Brr Brr.

I listened to the ringing. I imagined Grandma getting up off the settee and coming into the hall to answer it. She always had her apron on, even when she wasn't baking.

My throat felt all swollen up but when I actually touched it, it was still the normal size.

Brr Brr. Brr Brr.

'Hello?'

It wasn't Grandma's voice. I tasted a bit of sick in my mouth.

'Who is it?' I said. Then I remembered what Miss Crane said about manners and how people like you more if you use them.

'I need to speak to my grandma, please,' I said. 'Her name is Gladys.'

'You've got the wrong number, pal,' said the man and put the phone down.

You had to put the money in before you dialled the number. I still had some coins left in my pocket. I put them into the metal slot.

Brr Brr. Brr Brr.

'Hello?' The man sounded annoyed, like he knew it would be me again.

'Is my grandma there, please?'

'Are you deaf? I just said, you've got the wrong number.'

'Where is she?'

The man sighed.

'How the hell do I know? The council said the old woman who used to live here was in hospital.'

My thoughts were all tangled up but I didn't have time to separate them out. I imagined I was a detective in the LVPD. I needed more information.

'What's your address there, please?' I asked.

'Five, Oakham Road,' he said. 'Don't you know your own grandma's address?'

It was a rhetorical question because the man put the phone down before I could answer him.

I leaned on the metal shelf and wrote down everything in my notepad. I recorded every word of the conversation and wrote '5, OAKHAM ROAD, MANSFIELD' in block capitals because that bit was extra important.

There was a little card on the shelf with a rude picture of a lady on. She did massages. I put the card in my pocket and picked up my notebook and pen.

I went for a walk down the embankment so I could think straight.

I wanted to tell Mum that Grandma didn't live in her

house any more. I wanted to tell her that she might be in hospital. Mum would know what to do.

Then I thought about Mum's face when she was scared of Tony. I thought about the bruises on her face and neck and how she never wanted to talk about Grandma any more.

If I could find out where Grandma was on my own, maybe Mum might secretly come with me to see her, without telling Tony. If I told her tonight, before I knew where Grandma was, she would say I had to forget about it. I didn't want to make Mum's eyes sadder than they already were.

It was 6.15 p.m. Still ages until Mum came home.

Time for some murder investigation.

I walked across the bridge and up towards the hostel. The best thing to do when you were trying to find stuff out about someone was to talk to the people that knew them.

The hostel was on London Road. It took me twenty minutes to get there.

A group of men stood outside. They weren't as old and scruffy as Jean and Colin. They still looked a bit scruffy but they were a lot younger and a couple of them had cans of beer.

They didn't even look at me when I walked by them, into the open doorway.

Inside it smelt of cooked cabbage, like the dinner hall

does at school, even after all the food has been cleared away. A woman sitting at a desk looked up.

'Can I help you?' she said.

'I'm looking for Jean,' I said. 'Or anyone that knew Colin.'

The woman looked at me.

'Jean used to be a midwife until her son got killed and she had a breakdown. And Colin was murdered,' I said.

She shook her head and looked back down at her papers.

'Just have a look round if you like, see if you can spot anyone.'

It was a big room and there were a lot of people in it. Most of them looked like Jean from a distance – you could tell they were homeless. They were all different ages. I walked round the edge. People looked at me but nobody said anything.

There was a man standing at the back, near the drinks hatch. He was dressed in a security uniform. He looked like he might be in charge. He watched me as I walked around.

'What are you doing here?'

I turned and there was Jean. She was slumped on a wooden chair, slurping a mug of tea.

I sat down next to her on the wooden floor and got out my notepad and pen.

'I need to ask you some questions about Colin,' I said.

'I've promised him I'll find out who killed him.'

'Promised who?'

'Colin,' I said. 'His dead spirit that lives in the river.'

'Oh, I see,' said Jean.

Jean didn't know the answers to most of my questions.

What time was he last seen? Did he have anything valuable on him? Had he got any enemies?

'No idea,' answered Jean to each one.

I shut my notepad.

Then she said, 'You could ask Old Billy, over there.'

She pointed towards the far wall, where an old man was sitting on his own in the corner. He had the longest beard I had ever seen apart from in books.

We did about the Amish religion in RE. After they are married, Amish men have to let their beards grow. They have no choice. I wondered if Old Billy was Amish.

When I asked him, he roared with laughter, like it was the funniest thing he'd ever heard.

'Oh aye, that's me allreet.'

Old Billy was Scottish. Once he started talking you couldn't shut him up and his accent was difficult to understand.

'Ken ya go git me another nice cuppa from oo'er there, wee laddie?'

I got him the tea. He wanted THREE sugars in it, which was mad. No wonder his teeth were rotten.

We had a lady come into school to talk to us about

keeping your teeth healthy. She wasn't a proper dentist, but she still knew stuff because she was a Dental Hygienist.

People think you just need to clean your teeth and that's it. But you are supposed to floss them and rinse them with this mouthwash stuff that smells like sink cleaner. You have to do it every day if you want your teeth to stay really good and last you until you are very old. We all got to keep our bit of dental floss, which I still have on my bookshelf in my bedroom.

I told Mum about the special things we needed to get for our teeth but she said she had enough to worry about and money didn't grow on trees.

Old Billy laughed and laughed when I told him about what sugar does to your tooth enamel.

'Och, I'll get the special tooth equipment when I nip oot to git me nails manicured, bless ya, laddie. Bless ya.'

I didn't want to write all his Scottish words down in my notebook. The way he spoke made my head ache and it would take too long to write it all down, so I decided to just turn what he said back into English words.

'Translate,' Miss Crane had said, when we'd done the same thing in French class.

Old Billy knew Colin well. They used to sit together in the hostel.

Old Billy laughed after everything he said, like it was all a big joke. Which it wasn't.

'Did Colin have any enemies?'

'How do you mean?' said Old Billy.

'Was there anyone he knew who didn't like him?'

Old Billy stopped laughing.

'He was scared of someone,' he said with a frown. 'But he wouldn't tell me who it was.'

16

WHAT LIES BENEATH

I raced home and pulled out my sketchpad.

I drew all the people I'd seen at the hostel. I even drew the security guard and the woman at the entrance desk. You never knew who people might turn out to be.

I didn't draw Jean because I already had her in lots of the evidence sketches. Nobody was totally in the clear until Colin's killer had been found.

There are two ways of drawing people. One is to sketch their faces like a photograph, so it looks exactly like them in real life. People think you are a genius at drawing if you do it like this. The other way is even cleverer and it is the way that Lowry drew faces, including his own.

You have to look at someone and really *see* them. Not the size of their nose or colour of their eyes, but what lies underneath their features.

Say you spot a man on the street. When you first glance at him, you might not see anything at all, just a regular face. If you look closer, it could be that you notice deep, scrunchy lines all around his mouth, from years of being sad. His eyes might look OK at first, but then you see they are red and staring and although he is looking at you he isn't seeing you at all. He is lost in a world of his own.

Another day, you might spot someone who looks mean and nasty but when you get close they smile and kindness shines out. This one doesn't happen very often.

When you draw faces the Lowry way, you are drawing their whole life, not just what they actually look like on the surface.

When I finished drawing, it was nearly time for Mum to be back from work. I started to go downstairs, but I heard talking in the kitchen. I went back into my room and looked out of the window.

There was a car outside. After a few minutes, two men came out of our kitchen and drove away.

When I went downstairs, Tony and Ryan were fiddling around with some plastic bags near the door.

'Christ almighty!' Tony's hands jumped when he saw me. 'How long have you been there?'

'I just came downstairs,' I said.

'Well, DON'T come downstairs again when your mum's out. You aren't welcome down here. Understand?'

I didn't say anything. I ran back upstairs and huddled by my window, waiting.

I tried to do a bit more sketching but my arm felt stiff. It's very important to keep your arm and hand relaxed when you are drawing or it doesn't turn out right.

In the end, I just did a bit of shading, backwards and

forwards, so it looked dark like one of Lowry's seascapes at night. After a while, I felt relaxed again.

At 8.25 p.m., I saw my mum coming down the street. She was carrying a bag from the chippy. My tummy was really rumbly – I was dying for my tea. I waited until I actually heard the back door open and close and then I ran downstairs.

Mum was in the kitchen with Tony and Ryan. They were sorting out the chips.

'Hello, Kieran, love,' she said, looking over Tony's shoulder. 'You OK?'

I nodded and looked at the worktop. There were only two plates out.

'Is there enough for him to have a bit?' she asked.

'No,' said Ryan. 'There isn't.'

'Do you want me to do you a slice of toast?' Mum said.

I had three slices of toast.

I was still hungry.

Mum had gone upstairs with Tony. He must have been really tired to want to go to bed that early.

I buttered some more bread and took a slice of ham out of the fridge. I took it up the garden and shoved it under the gap in the shed door. Tyson loved it.

'Good boy,' I said.

Dogs aren't really allowed the same food that humans eat. It can make them proper poorly. You should buy dog food that has the special minerals and stuff in that they need. But human food was better than no food so the rules could be changed for Tyson.

Dogs also have different intestines to us. Theirs are much shorter and are better at digesting meat.

Their teeth are all sharp and pointy; they hardly have any flat ones at the back like we do. God made them like that so they can tear meat easily. Humans just use a knife and fork. Really posh people even have special knives just for cutting steak.

I went back inside and stood outside the living-room door. I prayed and prayed that Ryan would turn his game off and go out, but he hardly ever did that any more.

It was because he was addicted to his Xbox. There was this programme on television about it. People don't just get addicted to drugs or drink, like you might think. Other stuff is addictive too, like playing war games.

On the programme, two American boys just sat playing all day and all night, like Ryan. They even slept in their gaming chairs. When they needed a wee, they had plastic bottles to do it in so they didn't have to stop playing. It was the craziest thing you've ever seen.

CSI re-runs on Sky would be on the Crime Channel now. When one ended, another one started. It was ages since I'd seen any. I used to watch them on Grandma's telly, even though it was really small.

Tony's telly was massive; it covered the whole corner of the room. Him and his friend carried it in one day.

They didn't even have to pay for it. They laughed and said they found it when it fell off the back of a lorry. There were speakers in each corner which made a massive booming sound when someone got shot. I wished I could watch stuff on it, but I wasn't allowed.

I waited in the kitchen for a bit to see if Mum came down, but she didn't.

At 9.23 p.m. I went up to bed. I sketched a picture of me and Grandma sitting in a big room with a chandelier like the Queen has. There was a coffee table with loads of snacks on it, even fish and chips. Tyson was lying on a rug near the fire. He was soft as grease and his back legs weren't stiff any more.

There was a massive telly on the wall, and me and Grandma were watching *CSI*, Episode 5, Series 10.

I even had the remote control next to me. It felt brilliant.

(17)

MEMORIES

I was sitting in the monkey-puzzle-tree corner of the playground with my sketchpad, watching the others before the bell rang.

The three big boys who'd thrown oranges at me by the river came over. The boy with ginger hair was called Gareth. I didn't know the names of the other two.

Gareth spat near my foot. I shifted back a bit so the spit didn't go on my shoe.

'Why do you come to this school? It's for normal people,' the boy with the baseball cap said. 'Shouldn't you go to the *special* school in Clifton?'

'Yeah,' said Gareth. 'You should go on the special bus with all the other window-lickers.'

They laughed.

The black boy kicked out at me and I backed up a bit more. They were getting too close to my personal space.

'What's actually wrong with you, Downs?'

'Nothing,' I said, and carried on sketching.

'Nothing a bullet wouldn't fix,' said the black boy.

'Or a knife between the ribs.' Gareth laughed.

They came a bit closer.

The sea sound was going to start – I knew it. I looked up high into the monkey tree's branches. I imagined I was up there, where they couldn't touch me.

Somebody came over to talk to Gareth and they all turned round.

I imagined flicking a switch in my mind so I could think in a special way. They hated me, even though I'd never done anything bad to them.

What do they like? What do they love?

My brain was just coming up with nonsense.

I carried on sketching, my drawing hand was working super-fast.

After a few minutes, gravel showered down on to my pad.

'What you drawing, spaz?'

Gareth snatched the notepad from my hands. My heart lurched. All the murder evidence was in there. They could destroy it and then I'd be back to square one and Colin's killer might never be found.

'Give it back,' I said.

'You forgot to say please.' The boy with the baseball cap laughed and waved the pad above his head.

The pages started to flutter, trying to break free. Soon, all my precious evidence would be scattered all over the playground.

'Rip it up, man,' the black boy said, laughing.

Gareth reached up and took the pad in both his hands.

'Wait!' I said. 'Don't you want me to finish it? You can have it when I'm done.'

Gareth scowled and held the top sketch up in front of his face. The others craned their necks to see.

'What'd you draw that for, dumb-ass?' said the boy with the baseball cap. 'You having a laugh?'

The black boy whooped. 'It's the Three Gangsta Boys, man!'

That's what they liked to call themselves.

'It's wicked,' said Gareth. 'You're not as stupid as I thought, Downs.'

He handed the pad back to me.

'Finish it and give it me tomorrow.' The bell went and they swaggered off. Gareth turned round to shout to me. 'Put me a couple of busty babes on there too, man.'

I looked down at the sketch.

I'd drawn Gareth and his henchmen standing, arms folded, looking menacing and hard. A crowd of skinny boys stood and looked up at them, like they were heroes.

I'd made Gareth's biceps about three times bigger than they really were and given him tattoos and lots of bling round his neck and wrists.

I'd sketched what they wanted more than anything else. To be admired by everyone at school. They liked people being scared of them.

A couple of pages under that, I'd sketched them when they were down at the embankment. I'd made them look even skinnier than they actually were and covered their faces with oozing acne.

I let out a big sigh of relief that they didn't see it, but I wasn't sorry I'd drawn it.

'The Three Loser Boys,' I said out loud.

I looked around. I was the last one out, so I said it again, a bit louder. They thought I was thick but I had won.

I was still laughing when I got to class.

We had a free period first, so Miss Crane let me choose what I wanted to do. I asked to go on the library computer. I got to sit at the brand-new one with the thin screen, near the window. It was great.

While Miss Crane did her planning, I looked up hospitals in Mansfield and found a telephone number for Ashfield Community Hospital.

I wrote it down on a piece of paper and put it in my pocket to record in my notebook later.

Google Earth is the best thing ever. You can type a road in and the special camera finds it from where it sits, right up in space. It can see the whole planet.

It zooms down and down from space until it gets to the UK. Then it whirls further down into the exact street you want to look at. It makes you feel like you are swooping down from space with it.

I put in 'Oakham Street, Mansfield' and watched it zoom in.

The camera stays in the air until you click on the little orange man and go down on to the actual street. You can even walk him up and down the road and have a look around.

Soon as I got the little man down there, I saw Grandma's house. I remembered it. It made me feel sad, because it looked just the same as it used to, but Grandma wasn't there any more.

I looked at the front door. I remembered how the taxi driver would leave the food shopping bags at the door. We had to keep going backwards and forwards from the kitchen to fetch them in. It wasn't like a chore – it was great. It used to make me feel all warm inside, like me and Grandma were a team.

First job after that was always for Grandma to put the kettle on. Then we'd have our blackcurrant and cream tarts from Gents, even before we'd had a normal meal at teatime. We made the rules and nobody could say anything.

While Grandma tidied up, I sat at the kitchen table sketching. People think art is about big things like nature and important people. But there was beauty at Grandma's kitchen table because it's where we laughed and talked and made plans.

Lowry painted family scenes where nothing much was happening. The parents and children just stood there. They were held together with a special bond you couldn't see, living their lives. Their faces just said that they understood one another like nobody else outside their family could.

It was just a feeling you got when you looked at his paintings. Lowry painted a little window into people's souls.

I drew me and Grandma sky-diving and climbing up mountains. Grandma loved it that I always drew her wearing her apron in everything, even though you're not allowed to sky-dive in one in real life.

When I looked up, Miss Crane was watching me. I felt like she knew what I'd been thinking. I didn't like that because it was private.

I am in charge of my thoughts. Tony and Ryan and the older boys at school can't say what happens in my head.

I didn't even smile back at her.

When her eyes went dull, I felt bad, so I said a polite thing to make up for it.

'Thank you for helping me with my work.'

She did a smile with teeth and her eyes turned sparkly again.

'You're very welcome, Kieran,' she said.

I looked back at the computer screen and hummed 'Who Are You?', which is the theme tune to *CSI* by The Who. Roger Daltrey is brilliant, even though he is massively old.

When I looked up again, Miss Crane was still watching me.

⑱

BETTER TIMES

I went straight home after school.

When I opened the kitchen door, Ryan jumped out from behind it and did a really loud, high-pitched scream right in my ear.

Noises that loud always made me feel sick.

He went into the sitting room and sat making up the little plastic bags, packing them into the toolbox, even though Tony wasn't there.

'Make me a cup of tea, freak,' he shouted.

I put the kettle on and went upstairs.

The dirty wash basket in the bathroom was overflowing on to the bathroom lino. Mum was always at work and Tony never put the washer on.

I took my school clothes off and put on my tracky bottoms and a T-shirt. I had to put a jumper on too as my room was freezing.

I went back downstairs and made Ryan a cup of tea.

He took a sip.

'No sugar, dumb-ass,' he said and spat it on the floor. 'I'll have a cheese sandwich while you're in there.'

I took it back and put the sugar in. I did a bit of foamy

spit and stirred that in too. It was a brilliant way to get Ryan back.

I got out the bread and butter and cheese. I took the tea and sandwich in. He took the plate off me and looked at the sandwich.

'What the hell is this? The filling is supposed to be *inside* the bread, you bleeping idiot.'

I wasn't going to stick around and put up with Ryan's bad mood. I had a better idea.

I ran back upstairs and put my sketchpad and pencils into my rucksack. It was easy to turn a bad day into a good day. All you had to do was think of something to treat yourself with, rather than do everything for other people.

Especially when that other person happened to be Ryan.

Although it was cold outside, it wasn't raining, so I set off.

I could hear Ryan shouting as I shut the back door. When I came out of the alleyway at the side of the house, he banged on the window. It was easy to ignore him.

It took me about fifteen minutes to get to the Lace Market.

In Victorian times, the Lace Market was at the centre of the world's lace industry. I got a leaflet from the Tourist Office on a school trip and it told you all about it.

It's brilliant that it is only fifteen minutes from my

house. No one else in my class is interested in coming here, which is crazy.

The buildings are massively high and made of red brick. They are mostly posh apartments now that you have to buzz to get in. In the olden days they were used as salesrooms and warehouses to make and store the lace.

I walked up and down a couple of streets, just looking up and around me. There was nobody about, which is how I like it.

The City Council call this area the 'Creative Quarter' now. There is a big art gallery here and I'm going to get some of my drawings hung on the walls when I'm older.

It was easy to imagine you were an English gent and it was Victorian times. There are still the old railings and gas lamps around which modern builders don't have now.

People from all over the world came here to buy Nottingham lace. Now it belongs to me.

I sat down on a low wall in front of one of the apartment blocks. It was a good spot for looking up the street at the tallest buildings.

I turned to a fresh sheet in my sketchpad and selected a pencil.

In Salford, where Lowry lived, he used to sit and draw, like me. During his lunch hour, he drew sketches of people and buildings, on bits of paper. Sometimes, he gave them to passers-by.

I wasn't going to give my drawing away. Nobody

round here would want it.

I knew how Lowry felt when he looked at the tall buildings that used to be warehouses and factories.

They made you feel small and a bit scared. But somehow, you still liked them and felt proud.

'Industrial areas', Miss Crane calls them.

I started to sketch.

I drew smoking chimneys and turned all the apartment blocks back into warehouses filled with the world's finest lace. I made the people tiny next to the industrial buildings. I blocked out the modern world and went back to Victorian times.

Lowry always drew factories because not everyone lived in the countryside and had picnics. When you live in a city, you get to like the outline of dark buildings against the blue-grey sky. It's a different sort of beauty. He called these pictures 'industrial landscapes'.

I mixed up the real with the imaginary, like Lowry did. I painted my own reality.

'Very good.' An old man stopped to look at my drawing, while his dog sniffed at my rucksack. 'Although you're not supposed to sit here, you know.'

He pointed to a sign next to me that said:

Polite Notice
Please do not sit or stand on this wall.

I'd finished my drawing, so I snatched up my bits and stood up.

'These buildings were here before you were born and they'll still be here when you're six feet under,' I said.

The man opened his mouth and then closed it again.

Old people think they can say what they like to you. But if you stick up for yourself and answer them back, apparently you are the one being rude.

Sometimes, the rules sucked.

I started the long walk home.

(19)

SKY MAIL

I dawdled a bit on the way to school.

When I got to class, Miss Crane was already turned round in her seat, looking for me at the door. Her face was shiny bright, like when her boyfriend asked her to marry him on Valentine's Day. Girls love that sort of thing.

She patted the empty chair next to her.

'Morning, Kieran. I've got a surprise for you.'

She slid a white envelope in front of me. It had my full name and the school address on it. In the top left corner was the red, white and black Sky News logo.

I couldn't stop looking at it. It was a proper Sky News envelope. You can't buy them in the shops, even if you've got loads of money.

Miss Crane slit open the top of the envelope nice and neat, with a letter-opener.

I got to open out the letter and read it first because it was addressed to me. Nobody else should open your mail; it's a private thing everyone gets to do for themselves.

Tony opens my mum's letters. He doesn't even wait until she gets home from work.

I opened out the letter. There was a big Sky News logo

on the top. If you ran your finger over it, it felt like it was stuck on to the paper, not just printed on it.

'Embossed,' said Miss Crane.

I read the letter just to myself, first off. It was so brilliant that I had to have a puff on my inhaler.

Afterwards, Miss Crane asked me to read it out loud to the rest of the class.

Dear Kieran,
Thank you very much for your letter.

I was very sorry to hear about the upsetting incident that happened near your home. I am sure the police will do everything they can to bring the matter to a satisfactory close.

Unfortunately, I am not able to visit as my team and I have an extremely busy schedule here at Sky News.

Thank you very much for your interest and I hope you will keep working hard at school so that you can achieve your ambition of working with us at Sky.

I am enclosing a signed photograph of me and the Crime Team.

Yours sincerely,
Martin Brunt
Crime Correspondent
Sky News

When I'd finished reading, the whole class clapped.

I looked at the photograph Martin Brunt had sent me. It had been taken in the Sky News studio, the exact same one you see on telly.

Martin Brunt stood in the middle of the Crime Team with his arms folded. His face looked like he was in no mood to mess about.

He had actually signed the photo for real. You could even see where the letters had pressed through on the other side. It was so weird, thinking that Martin Brunt had touched the spot where my fingers were now.

'Would you like me to get the photograph framed for you, Kieran?' Miss Crane asked. 'You could hang it on your bedroom wall.'

'I'm hiding it in my secret *Beano* annual,' I said. 'So Ryan can't get it.'

We had to put the letter and photo away then because it was time for Literacy.

We were studying a book called *Lord of the Flies* written by a man called William Golding, who is dead now. It was about a group of boys who are in a plane crash and get stranded on this island, miles away from any places, shops or people.

'A remote island,' said Miss Crane.

The best thing on the island is that there are no adults. Not even one. The boys have to manage completely on their own; they have to hunt for food and everything.

I would like this but I wouldn't want to have to kill a pig like they do in the book.

I couldn't eat my school dinner because my tummy felt all fizzy.

It was cheese pie and mashed potato, which don't really go together. My mind is strict about which foods match up. Brown sauce only goes with sausages and bacon. You have to put red sauce on other things. If foods don't match, I can't eat them.

It's Jamie Oliver's fault about the mashed potato. He got rid of chips and all the other nice things. If you stay packed lunch, you're not even allowed chocolate or crisps in your lunchbox because of his healthy school-lunch campaign.

When all the schoolchildren grow up, nobody will buy his cookery books because of it and it serves him right.

I went to the library after dinner but there were no computers free so they sent me back out.

I tried to be invisible at the end of the football field.

In *Harry Potter*, there is an invisibility cloak which is made of the hair of a magical creature. I imagined I had it on, and for a bit it felt like it was working, because nobody even looked at me.

'Nice ankle-bangers,' said an older boy I didn't know. He had his arm round a girl who was wearing a short skirt. 'Is there a new fashion I don't know about?'

The girl giggled and they carried on walking round the

outside of the field. The boy put his hand on her bum and she didn't even push it away.

Ryan has a word for pretty girls who wear short skirts. He calls them 'slags'. It's because none of them ever want to go out with him.

I tried to pull my trouser hems down but they wouldn't shift.

I walked up the other side of the field and stood near two dinner ladies who were talking. I wished I had my letter and photo from Martin Brunt to look at but Miss Crane was keeping them safe until home time.

At the end of the day, I put my letter and photo in my satchel and ran out of school. Gareth and his friends always hang around the entrance to the park smoking, so I went the other way, even though it takes twice as long.

I went straight to the phone box and rang the hospital number.

A robot answered. They try and make it sound like it's a real lady on the phone but the voice doesn't stop for breath and if you speak, it just carries on. You had to choose numbers for different bits of the hospital. I kept pressing numbers until a real lady answered.

'I'm looking for my grandma,' I said. 'Her name is Gladys Clements and she used to live on Oakham Street in Mansfield.'

She put me through to another number and I had to say the exact same thing.

'Do you have her date of birth?'

'No,' I said. 'She used to come to our house but Tony said she wasn't welcome any more. Then the man who lives in her house said she's been taken into hospital.'

The words were tumbling out all wrong.

'It's best if you can get an adult to help you and call back,' she said. 'We need more information than that.'

When I got down the embankment, Jean was sitting on her bench. I sat down next to her.

'Nice trousers, buddy,' she said in an American accent.

Normally it makes me laugh when she puts her funny accents on, but this time it didn't.

'Tell Auntie Jean what's up, me duck.'

She put a bit of her blanket over my legs and I let her, even though there was a risk a flea could jump on me.

I told Jean that Tony had banned Grandma from the house when she said he was a violent, stinking pig who needed castrating. She laughed and said her and my grandma would get on well.

Her face went serious again when I said Grandma wasn't living at her house any more. She was missing, and nobody but me cared about it.

'The hospital needs her date of birth,' I said. 'But Mum won't tell me anything, in case Tony gets mad.'

'Did you ever have a little party when it was your grandma's birthday?' said Jean.

I had a think. My eyes went to the left, like they do

when you are accessing old information that has actually happened. If Jean understood body language, she would know I wasn't telling lies.

I remembered once Grandma stuck a candle in one of our little cakes and the wax melted down on to the cream so we couldn't eat that bit.

'Yes,' I said. 'I sang her "Happy Birthday".'

'Was it cold or hot outside?' Jean went on.

'Cold,' I said. 'One time it snowed and we made a birthday snowman.'

'Sounds fun,' said Jean. 'Now, were there Christmas decorations up around the time of Grandma's birthday?'

I shook my head.

'Fireworks?'

Then I remembered.

'Grandma said when she was little, her mum told her all the fireworks were for her but really it was because it was Bonfire Night.'

'What a pair of detectives we are!'

Jean said to leave it with her and she'd see what she could do.

I told her about my letter and photograph from Martin Brunt. Jean thought it sounded brilliant.

I didn't get them out in case some of Jean's fleas went on them.

The river was rough and leaves were blowing around our feet. Even Jean's blanket didn't keep us warm. The ducks and geese had gone to their little homes in the reeds.

Colin's flowers weren't by the river any more. I didn't say anything to Jean about Old Billy telling me that Colin had been scared of someone.

To be a good detective, you have to keep some things to yourself while you investigate and check stuff out. Only, I wasn't sure what I should do next.

When this happens, you just have to think about everything you know so far until another clue shows up. If this was a television series, they would cut out all the boring bits and it would be more interesting. But Colin's murder happened in real life, so all the boring bits got kept in.

When Jean set off for the hostel, I started to walk home.

I went the long way round and cut through past the Spar shop. I stood by the window for a bit and watched my mum doing her job. She was good at it; she never had to ask anybody anything. She just got on with it.

I imagined the glass wasn't there so it felt like I was actually next to her and could even smell her perfume. I liked my mum's smell, even when she hadn't washed her hair. It made me feel safe and sleepy.

The bruises on her face were turning purple and pink. The thick brown stuff didn't cover them as good. It made my chest ache, so I stopped looking.

I wished I could show her my letter and photograph.

'See you later, Mum.' I said it out loud and sounded happy. I pretended Tony wouldn't take her away from me as soon as she got in.

⟨20⟩

THE RESCUE

They all stood outside our house.

Three men, dressed in black uniforms, with a big white van. Tony stood at the end of the alleyway that ran up the side of the house. He was shouting and jabbing his finger at the man holding the clipboard.

One of the other men was talking on a mobile phone.

I walked a bit closer but not too near because if he saw me, Tony would send me up to my room.

Some of the neighbours began to step out of their front doors to watch.

'What are you lot looking at?' shouted Tony.

He was madder than I'd ever seen him, even more than when Mum went on her work's Christmas night out, without asking him.

Mrs Cartwright went back in but the others just stood there.

Part of me wanted to run back to the Spar to tell Mum. But I didn't do this because:

a) it was interesting and I didn't want to miss it; and
b) it looked like Tony might be getting into trouble.

The men wanted to go up the alleyway to get round the back of the house but Tony blocked their path.

Behind him I could see Ryan's head. He kept shouting, 'Get lost, you're not having him.'

A police car came fast from round the corner. It had its flashing blue light on but no siren.

Three policemen got out. One went up and said something to Tony; the other two spoke to the men in black. They looked like they weren't in any mood to mess about.

I took a few steps nearer.

'Who's bleeping reported me? Some coward who daren't even say it to my face?' He shouted it so all the people watching could hear.

'We can do this the hard way or the easy way, sir,' said the policeman. His words sounded polite but the way he said them definitely meant he thought Tony was a loser. 'Either way, we need access to your property.'

Someone opened the back of the van and they lifted a cage out.

The cage was massive. I hoped they were going to put Tony and Ryan in it.

Tony and Ryan stood to one side and let the men in black and a policeman go up the alleyway. I crossed over the road so I could get a better look. They went in the side gate.

Tony was kicking the brick wall under the window.

He was going absolutely mental about it all. Ryan stood looking at the cage. He looked over at me once and blinked a few times but he didn't say anything.

I filed all the pictures away in my unlocked brain to draw in my sketchpad later.

The police car was mint. I looked in the window and saw the radio and a computer display. They even had a laptop in there for sending and receiving data.

Some of the men were coming back down the alleyway. One of them looked at Tony like he hated him and shook his head.

'Mind your own business,' Tony said. 'It's nowt to do with you lot.'

More neighbours had come out now. They were standing in little groups, talking. Some had their slippers on and one lady was in her rollers and dressing gown.

The police officers and the men in black waited at the end of the alleyway for the last man to come back. He was walking very slowly. When he got out on to the street, people gasped out loud.

I didn't realize Tyson had got so thin. You could see his ribs, even though I'd given him the ham sandwich.

He was very sad. His head was hanging down. He could only walk really slowly and his legs kept wobbling. I felt bad now for not trusting him. He didn't even look dangerous.

A woman shouted, 'You cruel bleep,' really loud. She

wasn't bothered if Tony heard her. The police and the men in black looked like they agreed with her.

Now I was closer, I could see the men's badges said *RSPCA*. They are the animal police. They make sure people aren't cruel to their dogs and cats and even snakes.

You can give money every month to help them do their job and keep animals like Tyson safe. It is called 'donating'. I'm going to do it when I am a top reporter.

They opened the cage and Tyson walked into it. He was no trouble at all. Then they pressed a button and a lift thing took the cage up level with the van floor.

Tyson didn't even growl and bark at the men. He just looked sadly at Tony like he didn't want to leave him.

The three policemen walked up to Tony.

One of them said, 'Tony Jacobs, I am arresting you on a charge of cruelty to an animal.'

Tony started shouting.

'It's nowt to do with anyone else – he's my dog.'

'Yeah, he's our dog,' shouted Ryan. 'Just eff off.'

Tony had to go with them in the police car to make a statement.

Some of the people on the street clapped before they went back inside their houses.

Ryan did a spit towards them.

(21)

NEW BOY

I waited ten minutes before I went back into the house.

I opened the kitchen door a tiny bit and heard Ryan's game blasting out. Then the noise stopped.

'I liked him, you know,' he said. 'Tyson, I mean.'

I stood outside the living-room door. It was slightly open but I didn't go in. I could see Ryan sitting in his gaming chair, looking at his hands.

'That dog loved me. I used to take him down the riverbank before he turned nasty and bit me,' he said. 'I don't know how it came to this. It wasn't my fault.'

His voice broke in the middle, like a dried-out biscuit.

'I think he'll be OK now,' I said.

'Watch this,' he went on.

I opened the door and stepped inside the room. It was cosy and warm. I wished I could sit in there sometimes with Mum and watch TV.

Ryan turned his game on again and started pummelling the controls on his lap. The screen showed the viewpoint from Ryan's gun. He was a big, tough soldier in the game and he got to do a lot of bad things.

I watched as the room filled with the sound of gunfire. Soon, guts and brains exploded all over the screen.

'Pretty good, eh?' He grinned, hammering the controls like a maniac. 'You better go up now. Dad'll be back soon.'

I took two biscuits out of the tin on the table next to Ryan and crept upstairs.

First, I did some sketches of Tyson's rescue mission by the RSPCA. I thought they'd done great but I still like the police more. The RSPCA can't do anything unless the police help them so they're not really in charge.

Tyson wasn't like a matchstick-legged dog. Lowry painted scrawny little beasts, where you couldn't even tell the breed.

'Mongrels', Miss Crane called them.

Tyson was friendly like Lowry's dogs but he was massive and you could tell, even at a distance, he was a Rottweiler.

I drew all the pictures that actually happened in real life. Then I drew one where Tony was cramped up in the cage instead of Tyson. He was crouching down, looking scared.

Tony had no food or water. Me and the RSPCA men were poking at him through the bars, with sharp sticks.

Tyson was big and strong again in the sketch and he stood on his two back legs like a human, turning the key in a big padlock on the cage door. He was getting his own back. I drew him fierce, not friendly.

After that, I ate the biscuits to stop my tummy

rumbling and wrote down in my notebook about ringing the hospital.

I took my letter and photograph from Sky News out of my satchel and tucked it inside the cover of my *Beano* annual. I was careful to make sure there were no creases in it.

I decided I would draw a really good sketch of Martin Brunt catching a very bad murderer like Raoul Moat, and send it to him.

At 8.16 p.m., I heard a car pull up outside. I turned off my bedroom light and looked out of the window. Tony got out and banged the roof a couple of times before it drove away. Men do that to each other as a way of saying 'See you later'.

I left the light off and curled up under my blanket. I liked to sleep in my clothes because it kept me warmer during the night. I heard the back door open and slam shut. I started to feel sick and shaky. I wished the police had sent Tony to prison.

I waited.

I felt as if I was to blame for Tyson being taken. I thought Tony would be angry if he knew I'd given him the ham sandwich. But he would have liked one if he'd been starving.

After a bit, I heard the back door go again and I heard Mum's voice. I wanted to go down and see her, but it's best to stay under your blanket when you are all shaky like jelly and Tony is in a bad mood.

'What are you involved in? What do these visitors of yours want?' I heard Mum cry out.

The rolled-up bits of tissue I'd pushed into my ears didn't make the shouting any quieter. I prayed out loud Mum wouldn't get any more bruises. I prayed Tyson would get better and be happy in his new home.

When I got to school the next day, I told Miss Crane all about the raid.

She took out a photograph of her two dogs. They were very cute black-and-white Staffies. They were both big and strong. One was a boy and one was a girl. Miss Crane said the girl was the boss, even though she was smaller.

Miss Crane carried on staring at the photo, even after she'd shown it to me. Her face looked strange and she said, 'I'd kill anyone who hurt my dogs.'

It made my tummy swirl a bit. I don't like it when people say or do different things to usual.

Miss Crane looked up from the photo.

'I'm sorry, Kieran, I shouldn't have said that.' She put the photo back in her bag. 'It's just that it really upsets me that people can be so cruel to an innocent animal.'

It felt OK then because she had gone back to normal.

'Tony said someone had reported him to the RSPCA,' I said. 'But he didn't know who.'

Miss Crane did a tiny smirk and looked out of the window. She didn't say anything.

I was worried about Tyson but Miss Crane said the RSPCA would find him a new home. They had people who took care of abused animals and got them well again, she said. Then the animals were happy like they used to be before they were treated cruelly.

I wished some kind people would come and take my mum away and make her better when Tony hurts her. I'd like to see my mum's smiley, happy face again and for her not to be at work all the time. Then we could do stuff like we used to, like walking and kicking leaves down the embankment in our patterned wellies.

'What's wrong?' said Miss Crane. 'You look upset.'

'Nothing,' I said.

'Shall we have a little talk about how things are at home?' she asked.

'No,' I said. 'Everything is normal.'

There was a new boy in our class. He came from a country called Uganda. He had the blackest skin I'd ever seen. Miss Crane said Uganda is a very hot country and so people's skin needs to be as dark as possible so it doesn't burn.

My white skin would frazzle in a second out there but Karwana's skin is OK in both countries.

The whole class was told we should make Karwana very welcome and help him as much as we could. *Did we understand?* Everyone said yes, but at break and dinner-time, some people were still nasty to him, even on his first day.

Carlton Blake said, 'Eff off back to your own country, Car Wanker.'

You should call people by their proper names. That is one of the school rules that everyone has to agree to when they come to Meadows Comp.

But hardly anyone listens to the rules around here.

22

MASHED GREEN BANANAS

At dinner-time, I saw Karwana standing on his own, frozen in the middle of the playground like a statue.

Someone kicked a ball at his head. He didn't even know to hide at the edge somewhere.

'Do you want to stand over there with me?' I said, pointing.

He didn't say anything but he followed me down to the bottom of the field.

'Thank you for being my friend,' he said, when we stopped walking.

I couldn't believe he could speak English. I can't speak any Ugandan.

'Swahili', Miss Crane called it.

He taught me you say his name like this: 'Kah-wah-nah'. You could tell he didn't like being called 'Car Wanker'.

'My name means *Born During Wartime*,' he said. 'What does your name mean, Keer-Ron?'

My name didn't mean anything. I wish it did. Born During Wartime sounded brilliant. I liked how he said my name, even though it sounded wrong.

Two girls from our class came over and touched

Karwana's face. He smiled and his teeth were massively white. They giggled and ran off. Girls can be so dumb.

People at school never like new kids coming, apart from if someone is really tough and in a gang. Then they are scared of them and try and make friends. They hate people who are from different countries, like Karwana.

They think once they live somewhere, it belongs to them. The Trent is my river but I wouldn't mind Karwana looking at it. What if the council said the embankment belongs to us and you and Jean can't sit down there any more?

I would go crazy because nature doesn't belong to any person – it's for everyone to enjoy. Two people in my class even went to Spain for a holiday last year because both their mum and dad are working and they live in one of the new houses, away from the trouble.

You can go anywhere in the world you want to, if you have a job.

'I am going to visit Los Angeles when I'm a top reporter,' I told Karwana. 'Do you watch *CSI*?'

He shook his head and smiled his dazzly smile.

Karwana was on second dinner-sitting with me. I showed him how to hand his token in at the door of the dinner hall, to the Dinner Bag. Some dinner ladies are nice but most are bossy if they think you're messing about, even if you're new and you don't know what to do.

Karwana was even worse than me for food that matched. There was nothing there he liked to eat.

'What's your favourite food?' I asked.

'*Matoke*. It is mashed green bananas, very tasty.'

It sounded gross.

'Do you like sausage and mash? They go together.'

He didn't know what sausage and mash was, until I showed him. He made a face.

He had a bit of chicken in the end but he said he wished he could have it with some *ugali*. He explained it was maize meal made into a sort of porridge.

I thought about what it would be like if I had to go to school in Uganda and all they had at dinner was mashed green bananas and *ugali* porridge and there was nothing there I liked. It was mental.

After school I went straight down to the embankment.

Jean was on the bench with her blanket. She said hello but kept her eyes looking at the floor.

'What's wrong?' I said.

'I miss him,' she said. 'We used to sit together in the afternoons and put the world to rights.'

She meant Colin.

Jean said she didn't feel like answering my questions about him.

'It's the only way we'll find out what happened,' I said. 'All crimes get solved like this on *CSI*.'

'Go on then,' said Jean, eventually. 'Fire away.'

'Was there anybody Colin talked to a lot? A man, maybe? Was he scared of anyone?'

'Nobody,' said Jean. 'Apart from the young man with the beard. He used to come down to see Colin now and again.'

My heart did a little blip. The best detectives run on their gut feelings. That means, even before you get any evidence, a feeling comes that you are on the right track.

'You didn't tell me that before.'

Jean shrugged. 'I forgot. Anyway, I didn't see Colin with him very often. They just used to have a little chat under the bridge sometimes and then the man would go away again.'

'Did Colin seem scared of him?'

'No,' said Jean. 'He always seemed quite pleased to see him.'

'What did they talk about?'

'Haven't got a clue,' said Jean. 'I don't listen to other people's conversations. I'd make a rubbish detective, wouldn't I?'

I asked Jean if she'd seen the man recently.

'He came down the day before poor Colin died,' she said. 'I haven't seen him since.'

It was a very important piece of evidence that Jean had only just thought to tell me. Questioning always uncovers the clues.

I ran through Jean's answers once more in my mind so I remembered everything to record in my notebook later.

'Can you remember what he looks like?' I asked.

Jean nodded. 'Pretty much. Why?'

'Wait here,' I said.

I ran home. It took me six minutes.

I walked through the side gate and checked that the living-room curtains were closed before I walked across the yard to the kitchen door.

Tyson's shed door was open. It was strange knowing he wasn't in there any more. I hoped he was settled in his new home with kind owners who gave him treats and took him for walks.

The kitchen door wasn't closed properly. I slipped in and went into the hallway. I could hear Ryan's game and smell Tony's funny cigarette smell.

I got my notepad and sketchbook from under the bed and put them into my school satchel.

I heard the stairs creak.

I stopped moving and listened. They creaked again.

Someone was coming up the stairs.

I felt like my arms and legs were frozen. I tried to stay calm and breathe but my chest was tight and it felt like I was being pricked all over with pins and needles.

My bedroom door opened very slowly.

Tony stood in the doorway.

23

THE PHOTOFIT

Tony didn't say anything. He just stood and looked at me.

I tried to breathe but I couldn't. I got my inhaler out of my pocket and had a couple of puffs.

Then he said, 'I wonder how those b*****ds knew about Tyson not being well.'

'I don't know,' I said.

Tony looked around my bedroom. I was worried he might look under my bed and find my letter and photograph from Martin Brunt.

'Got a nice little set-up here, haven't you? Contribute nothing and live off me and your mum.'

I looked at my feet.

'You haven't pissed yourself again, have you?'

'No,' I said.

'We were talking last night, about you. Your mum was saying how it might be best for you to go and live in a children's home. You know, for special boys.'

It wasn't true. It wasn't true. It wasn't true.

I took another puff of my inhaler.

'I didn't tell them about Tyson,' I said.

'I know that – you haven't got the brains. But you

might have told somebody who *did* tell them.'

'I didn't.'

'You can tell me. Who was it?'

'Nobody.'

'Ryan saw you up the garden the other night, you lying little bleep.'

He took a couple of steps into the room. The sea sound came a bit closer.

'I was only seeing if he was all right,' I said. 'He was hungry and crying. Dogs don't like being on their own all the time – it's cruel.'

Tony's cheeks started to go red. I shouldn't have said it, even though it was the truth.

I looked at his hands. They were turning into fists.

I started to shake.

The doorbell rang.

Ryan shouted. 'Dad? You've got a visitor.'

The sea sound whooshed into my head and I felt dizzy.

Tony turned to go back downstairs. Outside my door, he looked back at me.

'When I find out who told them –' he jabbed his finger at me – 'I'm going to rip their head off and do the same to whoever grassed me up.'

I waited in my room until the visitor had gone. When I heard the back door slam shut, I crept downstairs. Tony was back in the sitting room, filling up the little toolbox bags with Ryan. I opened the kitchen door really quietly and slipped out.

The cold air felt lovely on my face. I was all clammy and my heart was still pounding.

I shook my head: one, two, three, four, five, six, seven, eight, nine, ten.

The swelling-up inside my head felt a bit better.

A lady across the road stopped walking her dog and looked at me.

I walked past the Spar on the way back down to the embankment.

I watched Mum serving. She looked nice, even with her yellowy, purple bruises.

My mum would never send me to a home. When you have known people all your life, you just know for sure whether they would do something or not.

It was me and Mum for keeps. We used to do this special thing where we balled our hands up and tapped the knuckles together. It meant *Us, forever.*

We hadn't done it in ages. What if Tony had changed Mum's mind about me? She might rather have Ryan as her son. Mum and Tony and Ryan could be a little family. Tyson had already gone and I could be next.

I put my knuckles on the window next to Mum's till.

'Me and you for keeps,' I said.

She didn't hear me but it didn't matter. If you say it out loud, it still works.

*

'I thought you'd gone home to bed, you've been gone so long,' said Jean when I got to the embankment.

'Sorry,' I said. 'I went home to get my sketchpad.'

'You'll have to be quick. I want to make sure I get a bed at the hostel tonight. My back is playing up something rotten.'

I asked Jean a few things about the mystery man before I started drawing.

'Does he look like anyone famous?'

'George Clooney,' said Jean. But she was being daft.

When you draw someone's face, I told her, you have to think about what's underneath the skin. Their bones.

'Sounds horrible,' said Jean.

It was like putting a tent up without poles if you didn't work out how the bones looked underneath.

Miss Crane called it 'bone structure'.

When Lowry painted self-portraits, he always did them with mad, staring, red eyes. Tony has eyes like that all the time now too.

'He was thin,' said Jean. 'Like him that played Charlie and the Chocolate Factory.'

'Johnny Depp,' I said.

'Only not good-looking like that but his beard was similar.' Jean nodded. 'He had bad teeth and his hair was brown, not black.'

Jean was remembering lots of good details.

I kept showing her my sketch and she said, 'Yes, like

that,' or 'No, bigger nose, wider mouth,' that sort of thing. When it was right, I made my lines a bit darker.

Jean couldn't remember the colour of his eyes but it didn't matter. It was the shape and how they looked that counted.

The last thing she told me was that the man had a scar running down from his left eyebrow to just above his mouth. I wondered how he'd got that. It sounded awesome.

Then I remembered he was the number one suspect for murdering Colin and a bit of sick taste came up into my mouth.

When I'd finished, I let Jean look at it.

'Oh my God,' she said. 'That's him.'

Jean said I was a genius.

We were getting closer to finding the killer.

I could feel it.

(24)

MYSTERY MAN

When Jean had gone to the hostel, I stayed by the river to think.

My brain was good at putting things in order and coming up with plans. Grandma always used to say that I was smart in a different way to most other children.

This is how it went in my head:

- I wanted to see my mum.
- She was still in bed when I went to school every morning.
- She was at work when I got in from school.
- When she got home, she belonged to Tony and not me.
- I could see her when she worked in the Spar but couldn't talk to her because of the staff rules.
- When she left work, she was on her own for a short time. Tony or her boss couldn't stop her talking to me.

After I had thought all this, I had a plan to wait for Mum after work and walk home with her.

I got my watch out of my pocket. It was 6.04 p.m. One

hour and fifty-six minutes until Mum finished work.

I wrote down every detail of Jean's description of the man.

I looked at my sketch again. If a man walked by, I took a really good look at him to see if his face matched.

It was getting dark now, so I went and sat on another bench under a street light.

It was the time I usually went home and up into my bedroom. My tummy was rumbly and I had nothing to eat. I had no money left in my pocket and my piggy bank was nearly empty.

I thought about what it might be like to live in a children's home. The food wouldn't match and there would be lots of boys there like Ryan, who wanted to punch and kick me.

There would be no safe place to hide my notebook and sketchpad. My letter and photograph from Martin Brunt would be torn into smithereens and flushed down the toilet.

My whole body felt heavy and slow. I felt like I wasn't even bothered if the big boys came to beat me up.

When you are a teenager, your hormones do weird things to your brain. The school nurse talked to us about it in Social Skills. She said it was OK to talk to an adult if we felt bad or depressed.

'Depressed' is when you keep thinking bad thoughts all the time and never any good ones. I was being depressed.

Sometimes you wanted to be – it felt better than being happy when everything was rubbish in your life.

Sarah Lamb's dad was depressed. He lost his job at the Co-op warehouse and he couldn't get another one because he was old. He was so sad, he hanged himself in the spare room.

I wanted to ask Sarah what her dad looked like when he'd been hanged but Miss Crane said that would be strictly out of order.

They used to hang people in London on Tower Hill. It was like going to the cinema for people back then; they used to queue up to watch it.

Depending on how the hangman tied the knot, you could have a quick death or a slow one. The government and even the Queen allowed it.

Grandma said she'd take me to London to see Tower Hill. You can go to the proper Tower of London, where the kings and queens actually lived. There are real Beefeaters there and people used to get beheaded if they made the Queen mad, even for something small like turning up late.

The best thing to see is London Bridge, because they used to cut traitors' heads off and stick them along the bridge on spikes to teach people a lesson.

When I find Grandma, we are going to go to London. And when I am a reporter for the *Post*, I am taking her and Mum to the Ritz for afternoon tea. The Ritz is the poshest hotel in the world. They even open the door for you when you go in.

I drew a picture of London Bridge. In my drawing, Tony and Ryan had been beheaded and their heads were stuck on spikes. Me and Tyson were walking along the bridge and Mum and Grandma were waving to us from the Ritz on the other side of the river.

I drew people and boats on the river. I drew industrial buildings like Butler's Wharf, where the big spice warehouses used to be. I had dogs and ducks and smoking chimneys in my picture. Lowry's paintings showed me how to mix them all together, like in real life.

You can draw what you like in pictures. It makes your thoughts settle down and stops you from being depressed.

When my hands felt too cold to draw any more, I put my notebook and sketchpad back in my satchel and stuck my hands in my pockets.

I looked over towards the bridge. I could see somebody moving down there.

I wanted to go and have a look but nobody goes down there when it is dark but the druggies.

Druggies aren't like normal homeless people. All they care about is taking crack cocaine. We learned about it at school. You just take it a couple of times for fun, but then you can't stop. It makes you as thin as a skeleton and the long, middle bit of your nose rots away if you snort it.

'The septum', Miss Crane called it.

The worst thing is if the druggies share needles. Then they can get AIDS, which stands for Acquired Immune Deficiency Syndrome. If you get that, then you are up bleep creek without a paddle because there is no cure.

If a little kid picks up a needle with AIDS on it and pricks their finger, they can get it and die, even though they've never taken drugs.

I saw some more movement down at the bridge. I crept closer but stayed in the shadows.

My mouth felt dry and it was hard to breathe but I kept edging nearer. It was the only way to gather more clues about Colin's murder.

I saw a man. He was standing staring at the river in the dark and smoking a cigarette.

He glanced around and I ducked back into the shadows.

He crushed the cigarette under his foot, then pulled up his collar and walked away.

If he thought he was disguised and safe, he was wrong. I'd seen his face before.

It was the security guard from the hostel.

(25)

US, FOREVER

A group of big boys stood outside the Spar.

It was 7.55 p.m. There were still a few minutes to go until Mum's finishing time. I stood round the corner in the dark. I felt safer knowing that I could see the boys but they couldn't see me.

I didn't care that I had to wait for a few minutes. I used the time to think about why the hostel security guard might have been hanging around at the embankment.

It was possible he lived around here but I had never seen him before.

Maybe he had something to do with Colin's death. He would have known Colin from the hostel. It was the only thing that made sense.

The boys outside the shop had cans of beer and were smoking. Their laughing and shouting was making a lot of noise.

Someone shouted 'Shut the bleep up!' from an upstairs window of a house at the side of the shop. They just laughed louder and stuck two fingers up, which is another way of swearing without words.

When people make a lot of noise in the street late at night, it is called 'Anti-social Behaviour'. It always happens on our estate on nearly all the streets, apart from where the new houses are.

You can ring the police about it but they never come out because they are too busy chasing stolen cars. The police wish they could help more but they haven't got enough staff to go round. That's why they weren't bothered about Colin.

I looked at the new Police Crime Map website on the library computer. It covers the whole country and you can see exactly what crimes have been committed, on your own street or even near your school.

I put in our postcode. Our whole estate was covered in little circles. Each circle had a number in it to show how many crimes had been committed. A lot of the numbers stood for 'Anti-social Behaviour', 'Vehicle Crime' and 'Drugs'. There were plenty of other crimes too, but those were the most popular. I even found circles for 'Violent Crime' and 'Possession of Weapons'.

The crime map makes our area look really bad. But when you live here it's OK. I've never even seen anyone with a gun.

I wrote down all the different crimes in my notebook. I would like to see all the details of each crime, but you are not allowed.

I asked Miss Crane what her postcode was. Hers was almost like mine, but on the other side of the river in West Bridgford.

There were no crime circles on her street at all. It was proper boring.

The boys outside the Spar shop started whistling and whooping. They were doing it at my mum, who had just come out.

'Show us ya tits, darling,' one of them yelled.

It made me really mad. I couldn't wait until I was grown-up and strong. I would batter them to pieces.

I was about to run over to her when my feet stopped moving without my brain telling them to.

A man appeared from round the corner and stood talking to her for a few minutes.

It was the security guard.

Mum kept shaking her head and looking at the floor. The man was talking and holding his arms out, palms upwards, like he was trying to get her to listen to him.

In the end he shrugged his shoulders and walked off in the opposite direction.

What did he want? What was he trying to do?

I dodged back down the street to the end and came out of an alleyway, a bit in front of Mum.

'Surprise!' I jumped out in front of her. She brought her hand to her mouth and squealed. I thought she was going to be sick.

'For God's sake, Kieran!'

I wanted her to be happy, not mad.

135

'Sorry, Mum,' I said. 'Who was that man you were talking to?'

'What are you doing here? Have you been spying on me?'

I shook my head. 'I just wanted to see you.'

Mum sighed. 'I know it's hard. I'm sorry, Kieran. When Tony gets a job, it'll be different. I'll have more time.'

Tony wasn't going to find a job because he just lay on the settee all day and night, smoking.

I wanted to ask her more about the security guard, but you have to get people on your side sometimes, before they open up.

'A new boy started school today. His name is Karwana.'

'Blimey,' said Mum. 'That's a bit of a mouthful.'

'He comes from Uganda. He likes mashed-up green bananas.'

She looked at me sideways. 'You didn't tell anyone about Tyson, did you?'

'No,' I said.

'Truth?'

'Truth. But I'm glad he's gone to a new home now, because he was very sad.'

I really hadn't told a soul about Tyson, except for Miss Crane. But I tell Miss Crane nearly everything, so she doesn't count.

'I feel bad,' she said. 'But it's done now, so that's it.'

That meant there would be no more talking about it.

'I don't want to live in a children's home,' I said.

Mum laughed. 'You daft bogger, what's brought that on?'

'I just don't.'

'That's all right then, cos you live with us. So stop fretting.'

Her eyes stayed straight in front when she said it. It meant she wasn't lying.

I balled my hand and held it up.

'Us, forever,' I said.

Mum did it back and we touched knuckles.

'I've seen that man down at the hostel,' I said. 'He's a security guard.'

'Stay away from him, and stay away from that flea-ridden hostel,' she snapped. 'I can't handle any more complications at the moment.'

How Mum knew the security guard was another puzzle that needed solving. But the main thing was that Mum wasn't going to send me to a children's home, even if Tony wanted her to.

So I decided to let it go. For now.

(26)

THE ALIBI

Normally, when I wait for Mum to come home, it always seems to take ages. But the walk back together went really quick.

When we turned on to our street, I had to stop and shake my head one, two, three, four, five, six, seven, eight, nine, ten times.

'Come on, Kieran, I haven't got time for this.'

'Can Karwana come over one day?' I said.

Mum pressed her lips together.

'Not a good idea,' she said.

'Why?'

'Tony wouldn't like it.'

'Why?'

'He just wouldn't,' she said.

'I've nearly done my picture of the sea in Art class,' I went on. 'Mrs Bentley said I can bring it home.'

'That's nice,' said Mum. 'Go up to your room and I'll shout you when tea's ready.'

'I still haven't found my special pencil sharpener,' I said. 'The one from my wooden prize box.'

'Kieran, it's been months. If it was here you'd have found it by now,' she replied. 'What about the red one I bought you from the Spar?'

'It doesn't match,' I said. 'The other one was made especially for my box.'

Mum covered her forehead with a hand and closed her eyes.

'I've got more to worry about than missing pencil sharpeners, Kieran,' she sighed. 'Upstairs now and I'll call you down for tea.'

Ryan tried to trip me up when I walked into the kitchen but I saw it coming.

'You stink of piss,' he whispered as I moved past him.

It was ages before Mum shouted me down for my tea. My tummy had stopped rumbling in the end.

Tony and Ryan had eaten meat pie with gravy. I saw the cartons on the worktop.

Me and Mum sat at the kitchen table and had beans on toast.

'I like meat pie,' I said.

Tony came in to get another can and slapped me on the back of the head as he walked past.

'Don't be so bleeping ungrateful,' he said. 'Eat what you're given.'

He kissed Mum on the top of her head and she smiled up at him. But it wasn't a full smile.

'Best go up to your room when you've finished that, love,' she said, when Tony had gone back to the living room. 'We don't want to get him in a mood again.'

'I haven't got any money in my piggy bank,' I said. 'Me and Karwana want to go out on the bus one day.'

Mum stood up and checked nobody was outside the kitchen door. Then she went to her bag and gave me three pounds.

'Keep that to yourself,' she said, and tapped her nose. 'It's nice you've got a little friend, even if he is foreign.'

It was only a bit of a lie because the money really was for the bus fare. Not with Karwana, though. It was to get me to Mansfield to see Grandma when I found her. I had left it with Jean like she'd told me to, but she hadn't said anything about it yet.

I remembered my letter and photograph from Martin Brunt.

'I'll fetch them and show you,' I said to Mum.

'Another time, Kieran,' she said. 'I've got things to do.'

I kissed Mum goodnight and went upstairs. It was 9.58 p.m.

I felt like I was swimming in mud when I moved. Even shaking my head didn't help. Everything was changing.

I curled up under my blankets in the dark with my clothes on. My hands were cold so I put them inside my shirt, next to my warm tummy.

Ryan had turned his game off and they were all watching telly. I could still hear it through the floor but it wasn't as loud as the Xbox.

I didn't see why I couldn't stay down to watch it if I was quiet and didn't get Tony in a mood.

I couldn't get to sleep.

The man's face, who Jean said looked like Johnny Depp, floated in front of my eyes.

He was out there somewhere. I just had to figure out how I could find him.

Then the security guard's face popped up. Why was he down at the embankment? And what had he been saying to Mum? Maybe he wanted her to be his alibi.

An 'alibi' is an excuse. It is a way of proving to the police that you aren't guilty of a crime. If the security guard convinced Mum to say she was with him on the day Colin was murdered, she would be his alibi and they'd have to let him go. Even though it would all be lies.

I needed to work out what both the men's connection had been with Colin.

My brain was like minestrone soup with all different bits floating in it that didn't make any sense.

As I fell asleep, I saw Tyson running in a meadow with daisies in it. He was happy and strong and you couldn't see his ribs any more.

There were no people there to hurt him.

THE MISSING MEDAL

'Keer-Ron, why do you have your own teacher?' Karwana asked me at break.

'Miss Crane is a teaching assistant. She helps me sometimes.'

'Why?'

I looked at his face up close. His black skin glistened. His hair had the tiniest curls you ever saw, very close to his head. I liked his eyes. They were deep brown, like a chocolate digestive, and they looked kind.

'I'm a bit different to the other people in my class. But not really bad, like Thomas Wheatley in Class Eight. He can't stop touching girls' tights.'

Thomas Wheatley was a genius at Maths and had already had a letter from Oxford University asking him to go there when he was grown-up. I would rather be good at drawing as it is more useful, especially when you are investigating a murder.

Karwana didn't say anything.

'Why did you leave Uganda?' I said.

His eyes went far away.

'It used to be nice there but not any more,' he said.

'Was your street full of crime circles?' I asked.

He shook his head.

'Government troops killed my father,' he said. 'They shot him in the head in front of me and my mother.'

A tear slid down his cheek and he looked away. I pretended I hadn't noticed.

I wanted to ask him what his father's brains looked like and if they went all over the wall but I didn't.

When I told Miss Crane, she said I had done very well to think before I spoke and it showed I was getting much better at understanding other people. But it didn't stop me wondering about it all the time.

Karwana wasn't scared of anyone at school, not even Gareth and his gang. He walked around, powerful and brave, like he was the King of Uganda.

'When you have faced soldiers with guns and machetes,' he said, 'silly boys like this hold no threat. They pretend they are big and brave, but underneath they are just afraid, like everyone else.'

After school I went down to the embankment to see Jean. She said I could go to the hostel with her to show Old Billy the drawing of the mystery man.

Sometimes, during an investigation, there are places that you have to go to which are unavoidable.

Mum had told me I wasn't to go to the hostel, but it was an unavoidable place. The clue to Colin's killer might well be found there. If I caught the killer, Mum would understand why I went there, and let me off.

It was busy at the hostel because it was going to be a cold night. Jean said it would be better if I sneaked in when the woman on the desk wasn't looking.

When there were a few people waiting to be registered, I slipped past and walked into the main room. Old Billy saw me straight away and put his hand up. I went to sit next to him.

'Noo then, have ye found any more clues aboot ya friend, laddie?'

'Yes,' I said, opening my satchel. 'I'd like you to take a look at this photofit and see if you recognize the man.'

Old Billy sat laughing under his breath. He didn't even say anything, he just kept laughing at whatever it was that he was thinking in his head.

I felt annoyed, like he didn't believe I could find the killer.

When I showed him my sketch, he stopped laughing.

'Did you draw that?' he said.

'Have you seen this man before?'

Old Billy looked a bit closer, then he turned the pad a bit and looked at it far away.

'No,' he said. 'I've never seen him before.'

Jean brought me over a bowl of soup. I looked up and the security guard was watching me. He didn't smile properly but the ends of his mouth went up a tiny bit.

I really wanted to ask him what he'd been doing down

at the embankment and what he'd been talking to my mum about, but I pulled my eyes away and ate my soup. Timing was everything and I didn't want to let on I'd spotted him the day before.

Jean got up and went over to see a lady in a white coat who had just walked into the room.

It was lovely having some tea when you were hungry. I liked coming here with Jean. Even sitting with Old Billy was better than being on my own on the bench at the embankment.

The hostel smelt a bit like dirty old socks, but once you got used to it, you didn't notice as much.

'Did you know that Colin was a hero fireman?' I said to Old Billy.

'Aye, that I did, lad. Very proud of his Medal of Bravery he was too.'

'Where is it?'

'What?'

'His Medal of Bravery?'

'Och, he carried it around in that stripy bag of his. Kept it wrapped in its tissue box and everything.' Old Billy stared in front of him but he wasn't really looking at anything. 'They'd engraved it with his name and the date. It meant the world to him, but what good is it now?'

This was very interesting. I had seen the contents of Colin's bag spread out on the riverbank by the police and there hadn't been a medal there.

I took out my notebook and wrote it down.

Old Billy did his funny, secret laugh again but I just ignored him.

The room was filling up with people for the night. The beds were through a door at the back. They were in what's called a 'dormitory'. Homeless people don't get a private room each. They have to share.

Jean showed it to me once. The beds were all lined up in rows, like how army soldiers sleep or sick people in the hospital. The women have one room and the men sleep in another.

I was going to tell Old Billy about my letter and photograph from Martin Brunt, but he wouldn't know who he was and that would take the excitement away.

'Would you go and get this poor old man a wee cup o' tea, please, laddie?'

Sometimes old people think you should do all their errands just because you are younger than them. Jean wasn't like that and my grandma wasn't either. I think old men might be lazier, but nobody has proved it yet.

I walked over to the drinks hatch.

The security guard stood next to it. He nodded at me.

He was about Tony's age but he had a kind face.

'I'm just getting a drink for Old Billy,' I said, in case he thought I was taking the homeless people's tea for myself.

'That old goat will have you running around,' he

laughed. He put his hand out to shake mine. 'Stephen. What's your name?'

'Kieran,' I said, and shook his hand.

He seemed OK but he looked at me a bit funny. Like he was making his mind up about something.

I thought about some of the police talks we'd had at school about perverts. Perverts could be anyone. Men, women, or even security guards.

They pretend to be your friend and then they try and put their hand down your trousers. Or up your skirt, if you are a girl. That's why you have to guard your personal space.

I snatched my hand away.

'Did you know a homeless man called Colin?' I said.

Stephen shook his head.

He swept his arm around the room. 'A lot of people use this place.'

'Do you live around here?' I said it like I wasn't really interested. You should always aim to sound casual and slightly disinterested when trying to trip up a perp.

'Not far away,' he said. 'You?'

If he knew my mum, he probably knew I was her son. He was playing silly games.

'I live in the Meadows,' I said. 'My mum works at the Spar shop there.'

I watched him carefully. I waited for him to reveal signs of nervousness or lying.

He watched me back.

I decided to take control of the situation.

'What were you talking to my mum about last night?'

I saw shock flash over his face for just a second, and then he looked away.

'You'll have to ask your mum about that,' he said. 'It's not my place to say.'

I got Old Billy's tea and took it over without looking at Stephen again.

There was something very suspicious about his behaviour, but him talking to my mum probably wasn't connected to Colin's murder. I knew this because my mum wouldn't ever hurt a homeless old man.

'You're a wee gem,' said Old Billy.

'I don't want to get you anything else,' I said, and fastened up my satchel.

I saw him do a face at me by pulling his chin down long.

Jean came back over and sat down next to me. She put her hand on my arm.

I didn't mind because I know Jean well.

'Kieran,' she said. 'I know where your grandma is.'

(28)

FOLLOWING CLUES

Jean knew the lady in the white coat. She was a volunteer doctor that came to the homeless shelter regularly, to help the people there.

'Dr Craig knew me when I was a midwife,' she said. 'She was quite happy to do me a favour and check your grandma's details out.'

The polite part of my brain thought I should kiss Jean, but I don't kiss people. Only Mum, on her cheek sometimes. And, of course, I used to kiss Grandma.

'Thank you very much for helping me, Jean,' I said instead. Polite words coming out of my mouth always sounded like they belonged to someone else.

'You're very welcome, lad. She's in the Ashfield Community Hospital, Ward Six B.'

'What's wrong with her?' I said.

'Dr Craig didn't say – they're not allowed to.'

I felt the crack in my heart get a bit bigger.

'I want to go and see her,' I said.

'I'll come with you if you like,' said Jean. 'We can go tomorrow after you finish school.'

Loads of people bunk off school just because they don't want to do lessons. I wished I could bunk off

149

tomorrow and go and see Grandma. It was important. More important than fractions and stupid PE.

If I didn't go, Miss Crane would ring my mum and ask where I was. Having your own teaching assistant sucked. You never got a minute's peace.

'I could come wi' ye both,' said Old Billy.

I didn't answer him and neither did Jean.

I wrote the hospital details about Grandma down in my notebook and put my coat on. Then I remembered about Colin's medal. I asked Jean if she'd seen it.

'Oh yes, he was always polishing it and showing it off,' she said. 'It was all he had left of his old life.'

'It wasn't in his bag,' I said. 'I would have seen it.'

'Maybe the police gave it to his family?' said Jean.

'But what if they didn't?' I asked.

'I'll get someone here to ring the police so I can report it missing, just in case.'

She smiled at me.

I said goodbye and walked towards the door. I didn't look at Stephen when I walked past him, in case he was some kind of a pervert.

I passed the lady at the desk on the way out.

'I didn't see you come in,' she said, frowning.

'I was looking for my grandma,' I said. Which is true.

It was cold and dark outside. I stuck to the main roads while I walked home. This is the best way you can keep safe. If you show you are nervous, you are more likely to get attacked. So I swung my arms as I walked, to show I wasn't scared, in case any criminals were watching.

I walked past KFC. It smelt lovely. I had the three pounds Mum gave me in my pocket, but that was for the bus fare to the hospital, so I couldn't spend it. A lady and a man came out and put a bag in the litter bin. It looked like it still had food in it.

I'd seen homeless people look in bins before and get food out. I'd never seen Jean do it, though.

I got near the bin. I looked at the brown paper bag poking out of the top. If people had just put it in there, it wouldn't be as bad as eating old, cold food.

Then one of the men from the shop came outside so I walked past the bin without stopping. When I was a reporter for the *Post* I would be able to eat as much KFC as I wanted.

Or McDonald's. It would be my choice.

We are always doing about the environment at school. Here's a gross fact about the environment: McDonald's cows are causing a load of damage to the ozone layer because of all their FARTS.

It's true. McDonald's have so many cows that their farting is making tonnes of carbon dioxide, which is called a greenhouse gas. This is very bad for the environment and burns a hole in the atmosphere.

We didn't learn about the McDonald's cows in class;

I found it on the computer one dinner time. I told Miss Crane about it, but I said 'trump', not 'fart'.

A few years ago, scientists said we would all frazzle and would have to wear sun cream and dark glasses, even in the house. This was because they said the greenhouse gases would destroy the protective layer of ozone around the Earth, and the sun would burn us into little bits.

This hasn't happened. All we have is more rainy summers. The girls hardly sunbathe by the embankment any more because of the rubbish weather.

It doesn't matter because I still have the card of the rude girl that I found in the phone box. She is showing more than her knickers. In fact she hadn't got any on. You aren't supposed to look at stuff like that but you can't help it when you get it out of your pocket by mistake.

When I trusted Karwana a bit more, I might show him the card.

If he promises not to tell.

29

REVIEWING THE EVIDENCE

I didn't want to go home.

I turned right instead of left and walked across to the embankment. It was dark and quiet and I was quite scared, but I still did it to dare myself. It felt different and exciting.

I walked near the river but stayed close to the trees. I had dark clothes on, like I was undercover, watching for suspects.

The wind carried one or two voices up from under the bridge. I made sure not to walk too close so the druggies couldn't get me.

The summer river is very different to the winter river.

In summer, there are more people around and everyone seems happier. Sometimes, students from the university take barbecues in little foil trays down to the embankment. They cook sausages and drink beer.

Sometimes a lad would see me looking and say, 'Want one, mate?'

Then a girl would say, 'Ahh, look at his trousers,' which has nothing at all to do with sausages.

My favourite thing about the embankment in the

summer is that the river has loads of boats on it.

The Trent Princess is a big party boat that goes up and down at night with people on it and loud music. Mostly, they do not even look at the river; they just drink and make a racket.

Sometimes, during the day, a big boat comes down the river with old people on it. They sit with cups of tea, watching everything that's happening on the riverbank. They like waving at you and are never sick in the water like the people on the party trips.

When I am old, I will go up and down on the river boats. I will pass the spot where Colin was murdered and remember how I solved it all on my own, when I was a lad.

The other boats that are often on the summer river are the rowers. Usually there are five or six men, or sometimes girls, in long rowing boats. A man sits at the front, shouting instructions at them.

'The *cox*,' said Miss Crane, when I told her about it in class.

The cox is in charge. He tells the rowers what to do and they're not allowed to say anything back. The cox shouts orders so all the rowers can hear. It sounds like he is getting mad, but he isn't – he just wants them to go faster, so they win.

You'd think that the rowers would make a lot of splashing when they come past you but they don't. They all row in time with each other and put the oars in the water at the correct angle.

The best out of all the boats are the 'Dragon boats'. There is actually a dragon's head at the front, and they beat drums as they race each other along the river. There are about twenty paddlers on each of them, and the cox sits at the front to time them and shout, 'Faster! Come on, team!'

Tonight, the river was quiet. I could hear some birds making noises, but I couldn't see them.

Somehow, it felt like stuff was going to start happening. My tummy felt like the inside of a cement mixer.

I tried to get the thoughts flattened out in my head:

- Jean had found out where Grandma was. We were going on the bus to see her tomorrow after school.
- Colin was scared of a man who looked a bit like Johnny Depp but was a lot uglier.
- Colin's Medal of Bravery was missing. It may have been taken by the killer.
- Tony thought it was my fault the RSPCA had come and rescued Tyson.
- It was OK because my mum said I didn't have to go and live in a children's home.
- Stephen, at the hostel, might be a pervert, so I shouldn't go near him or even look at him. But I still needed to find out how he knew my mum.

Miss Crane said it was always a good idea to write down what was worrying you because then you could sometimes stop the thoughts going round in your head. But it was too dark to get my notebook out and I didn't want to sit under a street light because you never knew who might be watching. I liked being in the shadows; it felt safer.

I looked up behind the trees and saw the lights on in the flats and houses. They all had people in them. Some would be happy and some would be sad.

You don't have to have a lot of money to be happy.

The people in Lowry's paintings are almost always poor but they look happy enough. Even the dogs look pleased to be there.

Tony gets money from his visitors but he's never happy. I've seen him counting it with his back to the kitchen door so he thinks nobody can see. It's not even coins. The people at the door give him lots of notes in thick wads.

He only counts his stash when Mum is at work.

He thinks he's keeping it all a secret.

30

SCARFACE

I wanted to meet Mum after work so we could walk home together, but it was too cold. My watch said 7.02 p.m. Fifty-eight minutes is a long time to wait. It doesn't mean I don't care about my mum.

I felt like my fingers were filled with freezing cold blood. They wouldn't warm up, even in my pockets.

It wouldn't bother a lizard because they are cold-blooded creatures. The brilliant thing about being cold-blooded is that you match the temperature of where you are at the time.

'Your environment,' said Miss Crane, when we learned about it in class.

If a lizard lies in the sun, it warms up quickly. If it is cold in the night, the lizard's body goes cold but it doesn't shiver.

Cold-blooded animals don't need as much food to stay warm and alive. Fish are cold-blooded. They'd have to be, living in the freezing Trent.

I looked at the black water. The street lights shone down on it and lit up the surface but it still looked like treacle. You couldn't see down to the bottom.

Fish were down there, swimming around. They never

157

stopped and they never closed their eyes to sleep. Fish were crazy.

I didn't walk by the Spar – I went straight home. I walked up the alleyway by the side of the house.

I heard voices, but before I could turn round I heard someone dash across the yard.

The gate smashed open and a man grabbed me by the throat. I screamed and my head banged on the brick wall.

'It's all right,' said Tony, laughing. 'It's only Steph's mongo son.'

The man grunted and let me go. My throat was killing me.

The man's face was covered in whiskers and he had a black beanie hat on. He turned to go back through the gate, and that's when I saw it. A scar, running down from his left eyebrow to the middle of his cheek.

'What are you staring at?' said Tony, clenching his teeth. 'Get in the house and up to your room, you little freak.'

I didn't want to go back inside. I wanted to wait out here until the man left.

Tony pushed me hard towards the kitchen door.

I went in and stood in the hallway. Ryan was playing on his Xbox. He was smoking one of Tony's smelly cigarettes and looked half asleep.

I felt sick and excited at the same time, but mostly sick.

I couldn't hear the exact words Tony and the man

were saying, but I heard odd bits like 'It's top quality' and 'Let me see the cash'.

I heard the man say, 'See you next week.'

Then Tony shut the back door.

I jumped into the understairs cupboard and shut the door. I went right to the back and hid under the old coats.

Tony came into the hall and I heard his footsteps stop.

My throat was so dry it made me want to cough. Then my breathing started to go funny, like when I need my inhaler.

The cupboard door opened. Tony pulled the carpet up. He lifted up a sheet of wood and put his toolbox in. He put the other stuff back.

If he looked at the back of the cupboard and saw me, he would go barmy and hit me hard on my head.

The noise of Ryan's gunshots got even louder and then went back to normal volume. Tony must have gone into the living room and closed the door again.

I stayed in the cupboard for another few minutes, just in case.

I've seen loads of films where the hero is tricked because the baddie pretends to go away, but really they are still standing right outside.

After a minute, I pushed open the cupboard door a tiny millimetre, which is the smallest stick on our school rulers. Then another, and another, until I could see that Tony really had gone back into the living room.

I climbed out of the cupboard and slipped out of the kitchen door. Then I ran down the alleyway to the end of the street. My breath was raspy and I felt for my inhaler in my pocket as I ran.

At the bottom of the street I stopped and took a puff. I looked left and right, but there was nobody but a man and his dog across the road.

Then I saw movement at the corner of Clipper Road as someone turned the corner and disappeared.

I ran down towards the corner. My chest felt tight, like guitar strings that were going to snap at any second.

If I didn't have enough breath, my legs would just give way and I'd never catch the man. I stopped again and had another puff of my inhaler

I turned into Clipper Road and saw him up ahead. He'd stopped to light a cigarette. I stayed where I was until he started walking again.

This wasn't pretend any more. I was actually trailing the killer. He might turn round at any second and see me. He could run back and stick me in the ribs or he might have a gun. There would be no witnesses.

I hung back a bit more and tried to stay in the shadows. Every time I got to a street light, I ran past it into the next dark patch of night, my heart pounding like a hammer in my chest. It was exactly like being in *Mission: Impossible*.

We got to the edge of the estate where it opens out on to the embankment. He stood still for a minute, then walked over to the trees where I'd been earlier. He was finishing his cigarette, looking out across the river.

He ground the stub under his foot and turned around. I was standing well back from the corner of the estate, next to a dark hedge where there was no street light. I knew all the smart tricks of surveillance.

He walked back over the road and turned right to where the flats were.

If he went into one of the blocks of flats, it would be very difficult to follow him without my cover being blown.

But he didn't. He walked past the flats and into the little dead-end road where the student bedsits were. Each house was split up into four bedsits, two upstairs and two down. They all had their own doors, with concrete stairs running up the side to the first floor ones.

I stayed at the corner of the road in the shadows and watched. He went down the path of the third house, ground floor.

He disappeared inside and the light came on.

The curtains were thin and patterned. They were closed.

I walked up the street, and stood across from the house.

I couldn't see him, but I could see his shadow and his movements through them.

The garden was full of rubbish and the path down the side of the house was dark and scary-looking.

It was the perfect house for a killer to hide in.

31

NIGHT VISITORS

When I got back home, Mum was in the kitchen.

'Where have you been?' she asked.

'I came to look for you at the shop,' I said.

I didn't feel bad about telling a little white lie. Sometimes you have to protect innocent people when you are investigating a crime.

Tony walked into the kitchen. He made a zipping-up-his-mouth action behind Mum's back. He meant about Scarface grabbing hold of me. He got a lager out of the fridge and went back to the living room.

I moved nearer to Mum. She was making cheese sandwiches.

'I saw the hostel security guard down at the embankment before he spoke to you,' I said. 'Did he know Colin, the man that died?'

She dropped the knife she was using and her eyes shot to the doorway. She was scared Tony would hear.

'I've told you,' she hissed. 'Keep away from Stephen.'

'Why, is he dangerous? What do you know about him?'

Mum put her face in her hands and shook her head.

'This is a nightmare,' she muttered to herself. Her

hands dropped away and she looked at me. 'Please, Kieran, forget it for now and I promise, when the time is right, I'll tell you everything.'

Mum's reply made me even more keen to uncover the truth.

What was the *everything* that she was going to tell me about?

Mum said to take my sandwich and my glass of milk up to my room. I didn't mind being on my own. I had lots of work to do to progress the investigation.

That is the official thing you say when stuff is happening all of a sudden and you have to get your act together.

First, I wrote everything down in my notebook. Then I drew a sketch of the man with the scar in his beanie hat and a close-up of Stephen's features.

Jean had done a good job of describing Scarface. My first photofit of him was a very good resemblance. In real life, he was much scruffier and his scar looked even bigger.

Next, I sketched the bedsit where Scarface lived. I drew the rubbish in the garden and everything. You have to make it look exactly like the actual scene, or you might miss some important evidence.

There was nothing else to do after that but get into bed and try to go to sleep.

My body felt tired but my mind was still awake and

jumping around like a mad monkey.

My thoughts raced round in my head like they were on a track.

Round and round. The killer. Round and round. Stephen. Grandma. Round and round. Tony hurting my mum . . .

I was asleep when my eyes just opened on their own and snapped me wide awake again. I pressed the little light on my watch, which I keep by my bed at night. It was 3.04 a.m.

I could hear voices outside my bedroom window. I got out of bed and sneaked a look through the curtains. There were two men in hoodies standing outside our gate.

They kept looking towards the house and then talking together, like they were deciding whether to do something.

I felt panicky inside. I wondered whether to wake up Mum and Tony. What if the men had guns and crept in? They might shoot Tony and Ryan while they were still asleep. I wouldn't mind this, but if they did that then they would probably shoot me and Mum too.

Tony had done the zipping-up thing to his mouth. That meant, no matter what I saw, I had to keep shtum.

I got out of bed and opened my bedroom door a tiny bit.

There was a knock at the kitchen door. My heart nearly jumped out of my mouth. *Boom, boom, boom* it went, sounding much louder than in the daytime.

I heard Mum's bedroom door open. I saw Tony come out, in just his tracky bottoms. He was holding a baseball bat.

He crept downstairs while Mum peeked through the bedroom door, holding her dressing gown together and shivering.

'Who is it?' I said.

'I don't know.' Mum's eyes were big and black in her face, where her eye make-up was all smudged.

'Go back to bed,' she whispered. 'Tony's sorting it out.' She closed her door again.

I didn't get back into bed. I stayed at the door, to listen. I heard Tony turn the key in the kitchen-door lock.

I waited to hear the shouting and screaming when Tony hit the men round the head with his bat.

'What time do you call this?' Tony said.

Another voice, speaking low.

'I don't give a bleep whether you're desperate,' said Tony. 'I told you never to come here after eight.'

More voices and rustling about. I heard him go into the understairs cupboard. Then Tony came back upstairs.

I closed my door quickly.

He went back into his bedroom. After two minutes, Mum and Tony started arguing.

I didn't pray any more that they'd stop, because it never worked.

'What are you up to?' I heard Mum wail. 'I don't want any trouble here, Tony.'

There was some banging about and then Mum started crying.

I put rolled-up tissue in my ears and the pillow over my head but I could still hear it.

Don't let him hurt my mum. Don't let him hurt my mum.

Saying it made me feel like I was doing something.

Even as I said the words, I knew he had already hurt her.

She always cried afterwards but she never got mad back.

32

THE FIGHT

I woke at the usual time, even though I'd been awake for ages in the night.

This is because every human has a special clock inbuilt into their brain. Even if you don't put your alarm on, your body clock will still wake you up.

The proper scientific words for the body clock are 'circadian rhythm'.

It's not just humans that have it. Plants and other mammals have one too. It's to do with light, and scientists have found it only works in Arctic animals when there are sunrises and sunsets. So, really, it is to do with the sun.

When the army want to get information out of suspects, they blindfold them. After a bit, the prisoners don't know whether it is light or dark and their biological clock switches off. Then they get all confused and don't know what time it is and tell them the truth about what really happened.

The army can get away with more stuff than the police. The police are not allowed to do things like that to get information out of people, even if they know they did the crime.

If a policeman shoots a man with a gun who has hurt people, there still has to be an investigation to see if the policeman did the right thing. It's mad.

My biological clock was very good; I never needed the alarm to wake up. Ryan's was rubbish; he never woke up until nearly dinner-time.

There's hardly anything that scientists don't know or can't find out. But they don't know every single thing in the world. They don't believe in things unless they can see them or measure them with equations and stuff.

There are lots of important things that scientists don't understand and can't measure. Like how much people love each other, or where love comes from. Or where it goes when people stop loving each other. And what causes gut feelings when you are solving a crime.

There are no experiments to prove these things exist, but they are still real, even though I'm not sure about the love thing. Sometimes, you just have to say it to your mum and grandma to keep them happy.

Lowry knew more about feelings than any scientist, even Albert Einstein.

He didn't need experiments to prove stuff.

He just painted pictures with five colours and made a feeling.

When you look at his paintings, they make your heart ache.

*

The house was very quiet.

It was the best thing about being the only one up, early in the morning. Mum wasn't crying; Tony wasn't shouting; Ryan's Xbox wasn't blasting out.

Today would be a good day.

It was the day I was going to see Grandma again, and soon everything would be back to normal.

I sat on my bed and looked through my notebook. My evidence notes were neat and organized. It gave me confidence that the crime would definitely be solved.

I packed it in my satchel, together with my sketchpad. I put my photograph and letter from Martin Brunt in there too, to show Grandma. It would cheer her up.

I emptied out the last few coins from my piggy bank and put them in my pocket with the three pounds Mum had given me.

Before I left the house, I wrapped up some biscuits and a couple of slices of bread in some kitchen roll, and put them in my satchel for later. I searched around for a pen, as I'd left mine in my bedroom.

There wasn't one in the kitchen drawer or on the side.

I peered into Mum's handbag on the worktop and reached for a pen that I could see was lodged down the side.

As I pulled it out, a birthday card was half pulled out too. There were three or four others behind it. Two had

170

racing cars on, the others had pictures of balloons and cakes.

I opened the first card. Then I looked at the others. They all said the same thing.

To Kieran,
Happy Birthday,
Love, Uncle Stephen x

My tongue felt swollen and dry.

It was crazy. I hadn't got an Uncle Stephen. And why would Mum keep old cards in her handbag like that?

I took one of the cards and slipped it inside my satchel. I don't know why I did it, but it wasn't dishonest because the cards were all written to me.

I unlocked the kitchen door and stepped out into the yard. The sun was shining and the sky was blue. It was still very cold.

I stood with my face up to the sun to let it warm me, as if I was a lizard.

The birds were chirping and I had all my stuff to show Grandma.

It felt brilliant.

It was still too early to go to school, so I walked down to the embankment and sat on the bench for a bit, looking at the river. The water was rippling and dancing about in the sunshine.

The coots were diving like crazy. The little white teardrops on their heads never got dirty, no matter what they did.

The Canada geese were showing off but I still liked them. They flew fast, just above the water, then they skidded down to a stop. All the other birds had to get out of the way.

You can tell the Canada geese think they're it, because they all swim together in a gang and stick their beaks in the air.

I looked up when a jogger came by.

'Morning,' he said.

'Morning,' I said.

I didn't even know him, but it made me feel nice to say it back. I liked early-morning people more than late-night ones.

I took the birthday card out and looked at it a couple of times. I only knew one man called Stephen and that was – *Stop it!* my mind screamed. *It's crazy.*

I had to concentrate on getting to see Grandma and solving Colin's murder.

'You seem in a good mood today, Kieran,' Miss Crane said, just before break.

I smiled at her but I didn't tell her why.

I even liked the lessons today. We had Literacy first. We had to be one of the characters in *Lord of the*

Flies and pretend to be on the island.

I chose to be Piggy. In my story, I found a special tonic made by a witch doctor on the island. I drank it and it made me strong and brave and I didn't need glasses any more.

I hunted down all the boys who had been horrible to me. The other boys wanted me to be the leader so I said yes. We captured Jack and Ralph, who are the bully boys in the book, and put them in a cage like the one the RSPCA men put Tyson in.

We gave them just enough food and water to keep them alive while we decided what to do with them.

Miss Crane told me to stop because it was break-time, so I didn't have time to get to the good bit where we started sticking them with spears.

That's how quickly the time goes when you get wrapped up in writing.

After break, it was Art. I finished my seascape and Mrs Bentley rolled it up for me and put an elastic band round it.

Miss Crane said she would collect it for me before the end of school so I could take it home.

I was going to take it with me to the hospital, to give Grandma. She could put it up in her house when she got it back. All the pieces were fitting together.

Karwana hadn't come to school, so I couldn't stand with him at dinner-time.

There was a computer free in the library and I got to go on it. I found the full address of the hospital on a website and wrote it down.

In the afternoon, we had French and PHSE. I pronounced all the French words correctly.

I put my hand up in PHSE when the teacher asked if anyone had ever been offered drugs, because I had. Under the bridge, once, when we first moved to the Meadows.

Some of the others in the class were laughing like they didn't believe I was telling the truth. They wouldn't laugh if they knew about Scarface and the murder.

As soon as the bell went, I grabbed my satchel and pushed my chair back.

'Someone's in a rush today,' said Miss Crane.

I walked/ran all the way down to the embankment. I didn't even need my inhaler.

I hoped Jean was ready to go. We could get on the bus to Mansfield that went past the Castle Marina Retail Park.

I'd just got to the trees when I saw two people fighting down on the riverbank. I watched as the tallest one got the other person round the neck and hit their head.

It should have been exciting but it wasn't. It made me feel all shaky and sick, like when Tony got mad with Mum.

The tall man pulled and pushed the other person. He was definitely winning.

I looked around for Jean. I saw her shopping trolley and bags by the bench.

I moved a bit closer to get a better look at the two people fighting.

That's when I realized.

One of them was Jean.

33

STOLEN

I ran down to the riverbank.

'Police!' I shouted.

The police weren't there, but it was the right thing to shout because the man let go of Jean and looked round right and left.

His eyes looked wild and his long hair was all stuck to his face.

It was a technique called 'bluffing'.

At school, if someone shouted 'Scrap!', everyone started running to the playground where the fights were, before they knew if it was true. Carlton Blake shouted it once when there wasn't even a fight and stood laughing while everyone ran.

Jean's nose was bleeding and she was holding her hand like she'd hurt it.

'Help me,' said Jean. Her voice sounded weak and she looked like she might faint and fall into the river.

'Leave her alone,' I shouted at the man. I copied Karwana with his strong, brave voice.

'Bleep off!' He snarled at me like a dog.

He took a step towards me.

'It's you, you little bleep!' He remembered me

from yesterday at the house.

When his face turned, I saw the scar.

'It's you!' I shouted.

He took off running then. He was scared because I knew him.

I also knew where he lived.

But he didn't know I knew that.

I took Jean over to sit down on the bench.

'It's him,' Jean said. She was trying to get her breath. 'It's the man who . . . Colin . . .'

'I know,' I said. 'I know who he is and where he lives. I've been doing some detective work.'

I dabbed at her nose with a tissue from my satchel.

'You might have broken your hand,' I said. 'You should go to the hospital.'

Jean started to sob. My stomach felt all twisted-up on itself. I'd never seen her cry like this before. Jean was tough and strong. This didn't match how she should be.

'He took my lad's ring,' she cried.

She held her hand up so I could see it was gone. Jean always wore a small gold sovereign ring on her middle finger. It was her son's ring. He even had it on when he died in the motorbike accident.

'He just wrenched it off,' she said. 'I begged him not to, but he wouldn't listen.'

Jean couldn't stop crying.

'Shall we go and see my grandma now?' I said.

It was like she couldn't hear me. She had her arms wrapped round her shoulders and was rocking forwards and backwards.

'We'll miss the bus if we don't go now,' I said.

Jean wasn't listening.

I sat with her for a while. I didn't know what to do.

'I promise I'll get your ring back for you, Jean,' I said. 'I've got to go now.'

Before I got to the road, I looked back at Jean. She was still rocking and crying.

I walked up to the main road and waited at the bus stop. The digital sign said the bus to Mansfield would arrive in four minutes. There was a lady already waiting.

'It's cold today, isn't it?' she said.

It was stupid politeness again.

'Yes,' I said. 'Pleased to meet you.'

She didn't speak to me again.

The bus came. It said *Mansfield* on the front. The lady got on.

The rule is that the first person at the bus stop gets on before you, even if there are plenty of seats. Miss Crane went through it all with me in Social Skills.

It was the same rule if you were waiting for a lift, even if there was nobody in it when it came and you could both fit in easily. You still had to let the other person go first.

I stood back and let the lady get on.

I stepped up on to the bus next. It smelt funny so I stayed at the door.

'I haven't got all day,' said the driver.

'I want to go and see my grandma at the Ashfield Community Hospital,' I said.

'Single or return?'

'I'm not sure,' I said.

The driver sighed.

'Are you coming back today?' he said.

I nodded.

'That will be two pounds eighty for a return ticket then, please.'

I gave him the three pounds Mum gave me and he gave me back a twenty-pence piece and a ticket.

'Keep your ticket safe,' he said. 'You'll have to show it to the driver on the way back.'

It was a shame the bus didn't have stairs. I wanted to sit up top, like I was in charge.

I sat near the back. It was 4.45 p.m.

I tucked the ticket inside my notebook and refastened my satchel.

At 4.55 p.m., I walked back down the aisle to the driver.

It was difficult walking when the bus was moving but not as hard as you might think it would be, because there are silver rails to hold on to, all the way down.

'Are we nearly there?' I asked.

The driver pulled a face. 'Are you having a laugh? We're not even out of Nottingham yet. We're due to get there about five forty p.m.'

'I'm worried the bus will go past my stop,' I said.

'Jeez, sit down, lad. I'll tell you when we get there.'

I went back to my seat. It was great looking out from the bus, once you relaxed. You could see everything. You could tell from the place-name signs whereabouts you were.

The bus went through Bulwell, Hucknall and Newstead. I even saw the great big wheel, the Headstocks, that used to pull the cages up and down at Annesley colliery, before it closed down.

If Lowry had lived around here, he would have drawn the big pit wheel and all the miners scurrying around it.

I saw the gates of Newstead Abbey. Lord Byron used to live there. He was a famous poet, and Grandma said he was a bit of a bogger with the ladies.

I ate a slice of bread and some of the biscuits in my satchel.

Then we went through Kirkby and Sutton. I saw the res. 'Res' is the cool way to say 'reservoir', like some of the boys at school say 'bro' for 'brother'. The res had ducks on it, but it wasn't nearly as long as the Trent; it was more like a great big man-made pond.

'Next stop is the hospital,' the driver shouted.

There were only two other people on the bus. They

turned round to see who the driver was telling.

I wanted to tell them I was going to see my grandma but Miss Crane said you shouldn't tell people you don't know your business, as they might think you were a bit odd. But when strangers spoke to me I had to be polite back. The rules were mental.

'Thank you,' I said to the driver.

I got off the bus and looked up the big driveway to the hospital. The buildings were massive. There were signs everywhere but none of them said *Ward 6B*.

It was a long way to walk up the drive, but I followed the signs for *Reception*. That's where you always go to find out anything at a new place.

I walked up to the big desk. It was very brightly lit and warm inside the big room.

There were lots of people around, some walking, some sitting. Some people looked up when I went in, and some carried on reading or just looking down at the floor.

'Can I help you?' said the lady at the desk.

She smiled but it wasn't real, like her boss had told her she had to do it.

'I've come to see my grandma,' I said. 'Her name is Gladys Clements and Dr Craig told Jean she is on Ward Six B.'

She looked at me.

'Have you got an adult with you?'

'No,' I said. 'I came here on the bus on my own.'

She tapped her pen on the desk like she was thinking about what to do.

It's not going to work. It's not going to work.

I did a bad thing.

'My mum is on her way,' I said. 'It's my job to find Ward Six B and ring her.'

The woman smiled, properly this time.

'I see,' she said. 'In that case, you go straight down that corridor, turn right, turn right again, and it's the third ward on the left.'

(34)

FINDING GRANDMA

I kept saying the directions in my head while I walked.

When the lady on Reception first told me, it sounded like it would be quick to get there. But the corridors were crazy long. It took ages to walk up the first one. Then I turned right and it was a great, big long corridor again.

There was once a man who *actually lived in a hospital* in real life. I saw it on the news. He kept moving around different areas, so nobody noticed he was there. He lived in the hospital for weeks.

At the time, my mum had said, 'That's stupid – someone would notice.'

But as I walked along I thought you could easily do it. Hospitals are massive, and in some of the corridors no one ever even walks past you.

I stood and looked at the double doors in front of me. The sign said *Ward 6B*.

I couldn't move.

I felt scared and happy, worried and pleased.

I thought about what it felt like, staying in my room all night while Mum was with Tony and Ryan. I thought about Saturday nights at Grandma's, watching telly and eating our treats.

The doors opened and a man came out pushing a trolley. He had a navy blue uniform on and a badge that said *Porter*.

I tried to get through before the doors closed.

'Sorry, mate,' he said. 'You can't just waltz in. You have to ring the bell.'

He went down the corridor, whistling. He seemed to like his job, but all he was doing was pushing a trolley round.

I pressed the bell.

No answer.

I pressed it again.

'Ward Six,' a voice called out of the intercom.

'It's Kieran Woods,' I said. 'I've come to see my grandma.'

'Patient's name, please?'

'Gladys Clements,' I said.

'Hold on.'

The doors opened and a nurse put her head out.

'Are you a relative of Gladys Clements?' She said.

'She's my grandma,' I said.

'How old are you?'

'Sixteen.'

Telling lies is BAD. Telling lies is BAD.

She opened the door to let me through.

'We didn't think she had any family,' the nurse said. 'She's never had a visitor.'

We walked into the ward. There were four big spaces that led from the main bit in the middle. She took me to the far one.

There were six beds in it. Some people had visitors sat at their bedside.

'Surprise, Gladys,' the nurse said, smiling. 'Visitor!'

She pulled back a curtain.

It didn't look like Grandma.

I took a step back.

'It's OK,' said the nurse. 'She looks a bit scary, but it's just the tubes.'

Grandma's eyes opened wide, and filled with shiny tears, when she saw me.

There was a clear plastic mask over her nose and mouth. She had tubes on her arms and even up her nose.

When I looked past the plastic and tubes, I saw her. She looked the same behind it all.

I touched her cheek. It was still soft and warm like before. Tears were running down from her pale blue eyes but she looked happy.

I took a tissue out of the box on the side and wiped her eyes. I did it gently as a mouse.

I touched her hand and found a bit of skin that had no tubes stuck in it. Her hand felt thin, like tissue paper stretched over bird bones.

When I sat down next to her, I held her hand properly and I felt a tiny squeeze. It meant she was OK.

I started to talk.

Grandma was pleased, I could tell. She sort of just relaxed back into her pillow and closed her eyes. She was still listening because sometimes she opened her eyes and made them wide, like when I told her about finding Colin's body and when the RSPCA came to take Tyson.

I told Grandma nearly everything that had happened.

I left out Tony hurting me and Mum, and also about the man attacking Jean. I remembered from Social Skills that when people are ill you have to think about what might upset them before opening your mouth.

When I told Grandma about Stephen being the security guard at the hostel and that I'd seen him talking to Mum, she did a strange little smile.

'She won't tell me anything,' I said. 'She said I have to wait until the time is right.'

I took the birthday card out of my satchel to show her. I opened it up so she could see the writing.

She closed her eyes and opened them again really quickly but it was longer than a blink and her lids looked damp again. She did another sad little half-smile and gave my hand a quick squeeze.

I had a feeling Grandma might know something about the puzzle, but she was trying to look like everything would be OK.

She squeezed my fingers loads when I told her about Martin Brunt. Grandma knew he was my favourite.

When you know people really well, you understand stuff like that about them that strangers don't.

'I've painted you a seascape picture at school for when you get your house back,' I said. 'I forgot to bring it.'

The nurse came over.

'Visiting time is finished now, love.'

'I don't want to go home,' I said.

Grandma squeezed my hand and blinked her eyes. It meant it was OK to go.

I kissed Grandma on her forehead. Her and Mum are the only people I have ever wanted to kiss in my whole life.

'When can she come out?' I asked the nurse when we walked back to the middle bit of the ward.

'She's been very poorly,' the nurse said. 'She had a big heart operation but she's on the mend now. A couple more days and we should be able to take out the tubes.'

I walked back down the corridors. I got lost twice.

I walked all the way down the main drive and waited at the bus stop opposite the one I got off at.

After about half an hour, a bus came that said *Nottingham* on the front. I showed my ticket to the driver and sat down.

I felt funny inside. Happy I'd managed to do this big thing on my own. Sad that grandma was so ill and had been all on her own.

I felt so proud of my grandma. She was small but she was strong inside. Her heart was cracked but she was getting better.

It was a brilliant feeling that scientists can't prove.

It felt more real than anything else in the world.

35

THE SECRET

I got off the bus and went straight to the embankment to see if Jean was there.

She wasn't.

I hoped that she had gone to the hostel and wasn't wondering around crying on her own, looking for her son's ring.

It was dark and quiet by the river. The word 'spooky' is an adjective. An adjective describes a noun: *The spooky river.*

Using adjectives is a good way to get lots of marks in stories at school.

I looked at my watch. It was 9.45 p.m. I wasn't always allowed to stay out this late. Mum was much more strict about when I came home before she worked all the time. Now she doesn't seem to notice.

Before I set off home, I walked up to the other side of the estate and crept up to the corner of Scarface's bedsit. The light was on.

I made a plan to come back tomorrow night a bit earlier, to see if he was out.

As I walked home, I heard shouting from youths on the streets a little way off. Before I turned on to the different roads, I stopped to check if everything was clear.

It felt like I was playing a game but it was real. If they caught me, they would do something nasty.

I had all my precious things in my satchel. They didn't mean anything to anyone but me, yet yobs would steal and ruin them if they got the chance. The incident would be just another circle on the police crime map. I don't know why youths around here enjoy doing that sort of thing to people.

In the day, the streets of the estate were OK, but at night they changed. It was like there were different rules once it got dark.

I marched along with confidence, like Karwana. These were my streets too; they didn't just belong to bully boys.

When I got back home, I turned the handle of the kitchen door slowly, so I could sneak in.

It was locked.

A bubble of panic popped into my chest.

It was really cold. If I slept outside, I might freeze to death.

Who would help Jean? Who would tell Mum about Grandma in hospital?

My hand seemed to take over, even though my mind said, 'Don't!'

I knocked on the back door.

I could hear the telly on as usual.

I counted to sixty, which is one minute.

Nobody came.

I knocked again.

I counted to one hundred and twenty, which is two minutes.

Then I knocked on the window.

The kitchen light came on and I saw Tony through the frosted glass.

The door opened really quickly, and Tony grabbed hold of my ear and pulled me inside with it. My ear was freezing; it felt like it was going to pull off if he didn't let go.

I heard myself yell. It sounded like somebody else was making the noise.

'Where have you been, you little bleep?'

He let go of my ear. It was throbbing. I touched it to check it was still there.

Tony pushed me back against the kitchen wall and I banged my head.

'I didn't know it was so late,' I said.

I could smell drink on his breath. His eyes were streaked with red and he smelt of sweat.

You are a stinking, sweaty pig.

I said it in my head, so he couldn't do anything about it.

'Are you smirking at me you little—'

'Tony, go in there, babe. I'll deal with this,' Mum said, grabbing his arm. She kissed him on the cheek. She gave me a secret wink to say she was trying to get me out of trouble.

'Get upstairs,' he yelled in my ear, so loud it was enough to make me deaf.

I ran away as quick as I could, to the stairs. Ryan jumped up from his Xbox chair and kicked me hard on the bum as I passed.

It hurt but I didn't let out a sound. I ran upstairs and shut my bedroom door.

I made a note of the time I called at the bedsit. I recorded the details of Scarface's attack on Jean.

I sketched Grandma in the hospital bed. I drew all of the tubes very light, so you could mostly just see Grandma's face. I made a map of the hospital corridors.

There was a tap on my bedroom door. Only Mum knocks like that.

I pulled a clean sheet of paper down over Grandma's face as Mum crept in.

'Just wanted to check you were OK,' she whispered, and kissed me on the forehead.

'I'm OK,' I said. 'I went in your bag for a pen and I found this.'

I pulled the birthday card out of my satchel.

Mum took a sharp breath and covered her mouth.

After a few seconds she moved her hand to cover her forehead. She squeezed her eyes shut.

'I'm sorry, Kieran,' she said. 'I didn't want you to find

out like this. I'd got all the cards out and put them in my handbag to show you the other day. I knew Stephen worked at the hostel, and it felt like the right time to tell you about him. I've kept all the cards he sent, every one . . . but Tony wouldn't let—'

'Have I got an uncle?' I said. 'Is that who you were talking to outside the shop?'

I thought about Stephen's face at the hostel. I remembered the way he had looked at me and watched me as I walked around.

Mum nodded.

'Stephen is your dad's brother.'

(36)

CAUGHT IN THE ACT

The next day, Karwana was back at school.

'My mother and I had to speak with a man from your government,' he said quietly. 'About my father.'

He said each word correctly but he still sounded foreign.

The fact I had an uncle was like a delicious secret that kept popping up in my mind every few minutes.

Mum said, if I wanted to, we could meet Stephen for a coffee one day after school.

'I want to talk to him about my dad,' I said.

But I wasn't ready to share it with anyone else yet.

I told Karwana about Grandma being in hospital.

'I am very sorry to hear that your grandmother is ill,' he said.

At dinner-time, we walked round the field together and I told Karwana about Scarface attacking Jean.

'Scarface may have stolen the ring to sell,' he said. 'For drugs.'

'Drugs?'

Karwana nodded. 'This is what happens in Uganda. When people need to buy drugs, they will stop at nothing. Even attacking an old lady.'

'I'm going to his bedsit tonight,' I said. 'To see if I can find anything out.'

'He may still have the ring,' Karwana said. 'I will help you search for it.'

I looked at him.

I wasn't sure.

I didn't normally trust people I'd just met. Plus, I felt sick when I thought about searching the bedsit for the ring. Going in there when Scarface was out might even be breaking the law, even though he was the criminal and we were the detectives.

'I am your friend,' Karwana said, as if he'd guessed what I was thinking. 'Friends help each other.'

I got the rude card out of my pocket.

'Promise you won't tell anyone I showed you?' I said.

Karwana looked at it and did his dazzly smile.

He whistled.

'Is this your sister?' he said.

'I haven't got a sister,' I said.

'Very nice and sexy, Keer-Ron.'

We both laughed.

Having a friend felt brilliant.

I gave Karwana the card. He put it in his pocket.

It meant we were properly best friends now.

'You seem to have had trouble keeping on task with your lessons today, Kieran,' said Miss Crane in the afternoon.

I couldn't concentrate; I kept thinking about going to the bedsit.

Karwana knew where the embankment was. He and his mum were living in one of the flats behind it.

We arranged to meet there at 7.30 p.m. on the dot. No being late allowed.

I went straight to the embankment after school. Jean wasn't there.

I wanted to go to the hostel and see Uncle Stephen. But it was weird and scary, as well as being exciting. And somehow, in my head, I couldn't make Stephen-the-security-guard into Stephen-my-uncle. It felt like I was going mental.

Instead, I went home to prepare for the raid on Scarface's bedsit.

A 'raid' is when the police search someone's property for evidence of a crime. The police have to have a 'warrant' before they break down someone's door or push their way into someone's house. I can't get a warrant, but when I tell the police why we had to search Scarface's bedsit they will understand.

I managed to get upstairs without Tony or Ryan noticing.

After a few minutes, the front door slammed.

I looked out of my window and saw Ryan going off down the street with his spotty friend, Reece. He'd finally finished all the waves in his game. I hoped and prayed it was ages until the next game came out, so I might get to watch *CSI* at least one time on the big telly.

I was doing some sit-ups on my floor to get strong for later when I heard the doorbell.

I went to my door and listened. Tony opened the kitchen door and shouted to whoever it was to come round the back way.

Something inside my head dared me to creep down the stairs.

Tony went into the kitchen and pulled the door closed behind him.

Except he didn't.

Pull it properly closed, I mean.

It was still open, just a tiny bit.

I knew Ryan was out, so I crept across the hall and right up to the door. I could see everything through the gap.

Tony's toolbox was open on the kitchen floor, behind the door. All the tools that used to be in there were gone. There were just rows of small plastic bags full of what looked like little rocks.

There was a man standing at the door. He had his hoodie pulled up so I couldn't see his face. He gave Tony some folded-up money. I could see there was loads of it, enough to buy a real-life racing car.

Tony counted the money, then gave the man a few of the little bags.

When Tony closed the door, I turned round to creep back upstairs but I tripped over the hall rug. Tony came out of the kitchen and stood there looking down at me.

'How long have you been there?' he demanded.

I couldn't answer him. The sea sound was whooshing so loud that my brain turned to mush and the words wouldn't come out.

Tony looked mad. His arms stayed down by his side but his hands were clenched into fist shapes.

He walked towards me.

'I said, how long?' His voice was quiet.

I stayed where I was and didn't move. I didn't even breathe.

Tony walked closer to me, and I could see his mouth moving. His eyes were squinted nearly shut and his teeth flashed like razors behind his lips.

He reached down and yanked my arm hard.

'Get up!' he shouted, so loud I could hear it over the thundering sea sound in my head. 'I'll teach you to effing spy on me,' he yelled, and stepped back. I saw his weight shift to one leg and his other foot lift off the floor into a kicking position.

I rolled backwards towards the stairs so he couldn't reach me.

'You little—'

He lunged forward, his fingers like sharp claws.

Then the doorbell rang.

His hands froze in mid-air. He looked back over his shoulder, as if he was trying to see who the caller was through the door. Then he straightened up and dropped his hands to his side. He unscrewed his face and looked like a human being again.

'Say a word about this to your mum and I will bleeping crucify you. Understand?'

I nodded and jumped up.

I ran up to my room, sat on the bed and took a few breaths of my inhaler. I could hear Tony talking to someone downstairs in the kitchen.

The sea sound was still there but it was further away now. I could feel my heart banging in the top of my throat, like it had jolted up from its normal position. This was impossible, but stress can make you feel weird stuff.

I wanted to stay in my room to calm down a bit more but I was scared that once his visitor had gone Tony would come upstairs and get me. There was nobody here who liked me, apart from Mum and she was at work. If Ryan came back, he would watch Tony hurt me, and maybe even film it on his phone, like he did when I had an asthma attack once.

I felt sure that Uncle Stephen would be tough enough to fight Tony, but he wasn't here either. It was important to get out of the house as soon as possible, because I didn't feel safe.

I packed my satchel with all my evidence and stood

at the top of the stairs. It felt like my guts had turned to paste and I felt hot, even though it was cold in the house.

I could still hear Tony's voice but his change of tone sounded like he might be getting ready to say 'See you later then, mate', like he always did before he closed the door and put his toolbox away.

Less than a minute from now it could just be me and Tony in the house, but somehow I couldn't move. I was stuck fast, like a statue.

Then a funny thing happened. Grandma's face flashed in my mind. She was smiling and well again and she nodded her head as if to say, *'You can do it, lad.'*

Mum's face joined Grandma's in my mind's eye, along with Uncle Stephen, Karwana and Miss Crane. I imagined them all encouraging me to move, to get away.

Tony might hate me, but there are lots of other people who care about me and want me around, I told myself. My feet started to shuffle.

I took a few deep breaths, and then I moved really quickly. I bounded down the stairs and ran full charge out of the kitchen and through the open door, pushing past the youth in the hooded top and nearly knocking him over.

I could hear shouting and yelling behind me but I didn't look back. I ran and ran, away from Tony, towards the river and Jean and the ducks.

*

I was an hour early for meeting Karwana, but when I got to the embankment Jean was back on her bench.

I was so pleased that she was safe, I couldn't stop smiling. Now I was by the river, all my Tony-terror started melting away.

'At least somebody looks pleased to see me,' she said.

'I was worried about where you'd gone,' I said.

'They looked after me at the hostel,' Jean said, 'let me stay there all day.'

I told her about Grandma.

'I'm so happy for you, lad,' she said.

I was pleased that Jean had stopped crying.

I looked at her finger but I didn't mention the ring.

'It's OK,' she said, when she saw me looking. 'The ring's gone and that's that. Like Old Billy says, my memories are up here.' She tapped her head. 'Nobody can take them away.'

That was true. I had memories of my dad somewhere in my head, as well. Now I had an uncle who might be able to help me remember him too.

'The hostel staff rang the police,' Jean went on. 'I told them about the man attacking me and I gave them a description of him, the ring, and also Colin's missing medal. They said to check the local pawn shops and gave me a special number to call if I see either of them in a shop window.'

'Is that it?' I said.

Surely the police would be more interested than that?

Jean nodded.

'If they don't give a toss about Colin being murdered, they're not going to come out here for a ring being nicked, are they?'

'Did you see Stephen, the security guard at the hostel?' I asked.

'Nah,' said Jean.

She rummaged around in one of her bags.

'Here,' she said.

She pushed a ten-pound note into my hand.

'That's towards your bus fares to the hospital until your grandma gets out,' she said.

'But, Jean—'

'Shh. Take it. Colin's family gave me thirty pounds and I haven't spent any yet. Me and you are friends, and friends help each other out.'

'Thank you,' I said, and put the money in my pocket.

I had the best two friends in the world.

37

SCARFACE'S LAIR

'This is my friend Karwana,' I said to Jean. 'He comes from Uganda.'

This is called 'introducing' someone. When you have two people who don't know each other but you are friends with both, you introduce them. Miss Crane taught me how to do it properly. It's to do with politeness.

'Very pleased to meet you,' said Jean.

Her hand was ditched with muck, but Karwana still shook it.

We said goodbye to Jean and walked back to the road.

Karwana looked like Spiderman. He was all dressed in black, even his trainers.

'In case I have to climb,' he said.

I wished I had an outfit like that. Karwana said he hadn't watched *CSI*, yet somehow he knew all about dressing in dark clothing so as not to be seen.

Karwana didn't seem one bit scared. It made me feel like I wasn't the boss.

Then I remembered that I had brought Karwana in to help with *my* plan. I had still masterminded it, like a lead detective. And I had all the notes and evidence.

*

We walked up into the estate and stopped at the corner of Walton Road. It was 7.41 p.m.

I showed him which bedsit it was. There was no light on inside.

'We need to establish if the perp is home,' I said.

Karwana ran across the road and disappeared down the path.

Two minutes later, he was back.

'Scarface is out,' he said with a grin. 'But you won't believe it: he's left the back door open!'

I felt relieved that we didn't have to break a window to get in. The police might still be annoyed that we were going into someone else's house to look for evidence without a warrant but someone had to expose Scarface as a criminal and maybe even a murderer. Even if they put me in prison, I wanted to do it for Jean.

I was glad I'd had nothing to eat. My guts were churning like mad.

Planning stuff was great but actually doing it was much scarier than I thought.

We went down the path.

I coughed.

Karwana put his finger up to his lips.

'Very important to be quiet, Keer-Ron.' He pointed to the upstairs bedsit, where there was a light on.

I felt a bit annoyed. You couldn't help coughing.

I took charge and used the proper terminology, while

in my head I said a silent prayer that the police would understand why we had to enter Scarface's lair.

'OK, let's proceed through the back door. Gloves on?'

Karwana nodded.

We crept up to the door and pushed it open, slowly. Scarface must've pulled it to when he left, not realizing it hadn't properly closed.

I hadn't remembered to bring a torch, so we put the kitchen light on.

Every inch of the worktop was covered in dirty pots and beer cans. Pizza boxes were scattered all over the floor. It smelt rank.

There wasn't even a drawer or a cupboard to search. Just a cooker, a microwave, a sink and a table.

We turned off the light and went through to the other room. It was a living room and bedroom in one.

'We'd better be quick in here,' I said.

I could feel my heart pounding in my chest and even in my mouth. Scarface could return at any time and trap us like rats. He might beat us or drug us and keep us prisoner here, where nobody would think to look.

'Keer-Ron,' hissed Karwana, shaking the horrible thoughts away. 'Come on.'

We started to search for Jean's son's ring. We didn't need to put the light on – the room was lit up with an orange glow from the street lights.

The carpet was old and filthy. My feet kept sticking

to it. We took the cushions off the settee and pushed our hands down the sides.

Nothing.

There was a wooden unit in the corner but no telly on it. Karwana opened the drawer and started looking through a tangle of wires.

It was the weirdest thing, being inside someone else's house.

The noises seemed louder and time went faster.

My heart was banging against my breastbone.

I looked under the settee and the chair.

Nothing.

Then I saw Scarface's beanie hat on the coffee table.

I picked it up and something glinted that was hidden underneath.

'Jean's ring!' I said.

Karwana was looking at something star-shaped in his gloved hand.

'What is it?' I said.

He opened his hand to show me. It was silver and gold with colours in the middle.

I held it under the light and read the glinting, engraved words.

'It's Colin's Medal of Bravery,' I said.

Karwana peeped through the curtains.

'Someone is coming,' he hissed.

My guts lurched up into my throat.

I tried to take in great gulps of air. I grabbed my inhaler and took a puff.

Karwana had locked the kitchen door behind us.

We wedged ourselves in behind the couch.

'As soon as he comes in here, we must run for our lives,' said Karwana.

I felt sure I was going to wee myself.

I stopped breathing.

Someone was unlocking the kitchen door from the outside.

'It is Scarface,' said Karwana.

Now he sounded scared too.

My chest was getting tighter. I tried to get my inhaler but couldn't reach my pocket because it was jammed up tight against the back of the settee.

'Stay calm, Keer-Ron.'

'It's my asthma,' I gasped.

We heard the kitchen door bang open. Scarface swore as he tripped up on something, coming in.

He snapped the kitchen light on and started clattering about in there. He was talking to himself but his voice sounded all slurry and you couldn't understand him.

'He's stoned,' whispered Karwana.

He slid out from the end of the settee. I wanted to pull him back but he had already gone.

It freed up some space so I could reach my inhaler. I took two puffs of it and my breathing got easier.

Karwana crept over and peered at Scarface through the tiny gap in the door. Then he tiptoed back to the settee.

'Come on, Keer-Ron,' he whispered. 'When I give the word, we run straight past him and out of the door. OK?'

I nodded. I'd put Jean's ring and Colin's medal back where we found them. If we removed the evidence, the police wouldn't be able to prove that Scarface really was the thief . . . and Colin's killer.

I crept over to join Karwana by the living-room door.

'Now!' Karwana flung open the door and we rushed into the kitchen. I stayed right behind him.

Scarface dropped his pizza in shock.

'What the—'

Karwana pushed him out of the way and grabbed at the door latch.

Scarface turned really quickly and hit me in the face.

I felt blood trickling down from my nose.

Karwana thought I was still behind him and ran outside.

Scarface grabbed me by the throat and started to bang my head against the wall.

'Why are you here?' he screamed.

'We came for Jean's ring,' I managed between gulps of breath.

'You little swine,' he cursed. 'I've got a special contact lined up to buy that ring and the old geezer's medal. Pity it wasn't a mobile or an iPad. They're much easier to get rid of.'

His grip tightened on my neck.

I tried to scream but my breath was draining away. I needed my inhaler.

Scarface's eyes were crazy mad and his face started to blur in front of me. The sea sound was roaring in my ears, his mouth was moving but I couldn't hear what he was saying any more.

I saw the shape of Karwana rush back in and grab something from the worktop.

He brought it down on the back of Scarface's head with a big crack.

Scarface's eyes went big and wide then he sort of toppled back and slid down the opposite wall.

Next thing, Karwana was pushing my inhaler towards my face.

I took a puff.

Breathe.

Another one.

'Are you OK, Keer-Ron?'

I nodded and wiped the blood from my nose.

'Is he dead?' My voice was all raspy.

'No, he is breathing,' said Karwana. He still had the saucepan in his hand.

'Come quickly. We must get out while we can,' he said.

38

POLICE ALERT

We ran out of the cul-de-sac and on to the next street.

I stopped to use my inhaler, then we ran again until we got to the edge of the estate.

Karwana had to go home.

'I don't want to go but my mother will worry,' he said. 'Will you be OK, Keer-Ron?'

'Yes,' I said.

I felt much better now my breathing was back to normal but we were both worried that Scarface could come after us

Karwana would be safe at home because Scarface didn't know who he was. But Scarface had seen me, and he would probably go straight to my house and tell Tony what I'd done when he woke up.

I knew exactly what I had to do.

'I'm going to the hostel,' I told Karwana. 'They will ring the police.'

When I got to the hostel, the lady on the front desk said, 'It's not a free-for-all here, you know.'

I used all my politeness skills.

'I'm sorry to bother you. Please could I speak to Jean or Stephen?'

She looked back down at her magazine.

'Don't take all night,' she said.

Jean was sitting with Old Billy.

'I know where your son's ring is, Jean,' I said. I felt all out of breath.

She opened her mouth, closed it again and then burst into tears.

'Ye haven't much luck wi' the ladies, laddie,' laughed Old Billy.

'I need to tell the police where to find it,' I said.

'Where is it?' She stood up and grabbed my arms which made me go stiff like I was made of stone.

'It's at Scarface's bedsit,' I said, struggling to get free. 'And guess what else we found?'

I told her about Karwana finding Colin's medal.

'That murdering toerag!' she cried.

Old Billy shouted Stephen over.

He came and stood next to me. He asked me what had happened, but I could hardly speak to him. Jean and Old Billy told him about Scarface's bedsit and he rang the police on his mobile phone.

I looked at his face up close. His eyes, his nose, his mouth. I wondered which bits of him looked like my dad.

He put his hand on my shoulder and walked me a little way from Jean.

'Your mum's told you who I am, hasn't she?'

I nodded. All I could do was stare at him.

'I've tried to see you for years,' he said. 'I wanted to be part of your life but it's been difficult for your mum. She's always been worried that Tony wouldn't allow it.'

I took a breath and forced myself to speak.

'I found your birthday cards in Mum's handbag,' I said.

'I sent you one every year without fail,' he said. 'Then your mum met Tony and we lost touch. I couldn't believe it when I saw you at the hostel.'

'Are you really my uncle?' I said.

He nodded. 'I've got lots of photos of your dad, and some of both of you, when you were just a baby. When this trouble is sorted out, you can come over and meet your cousin, Bradley. He's my lad.'

If you breathe in too much oxygen, it makes you feel light-headed. That was how I felt at that second. It felt like I was floating away from everything that was bad.

All the photographs that Tony had burned didn't matter as much now. My uncle had got lots more of me and Dad. It felt like he was real again in my mind and not just an outline with no filling-in.

'You're the spitting image of him,' Stephen said. 'No matter what anybody might have said about him, he loved you more than life.'

I was going to get to know my own dad again in a different way.

I wanted to talk to Stephen more about him.

I wanted to ask stuff like, What were his favourite foods, and what television programmes did he like to watch? What did his voice sound like? Did he like football?

Then two police officers came. One had stripes on his shoulders, which meant he was quite high up. Everyone in the hostel stopped what they were doing and watched them walk over to us.

The lady on the desk showed the policemen to an office at the back they could use.

Me and Jean went in, and between us, we told them the story from the day I found Colin's body in the river.

'Can you describe this man?' said the boss policeman. His badge said *Sergeant Bream*.

'He can do better than that,' said Jean. 'The lad's an artistic genius.'

I got my sketchpad out and showed them the photofit sketch and the second drawing I'd done of Scarface without his hat, when he'd attacked Jean.

'Are you trying to say you've drawn these?' The other policeman frowned. 'We haven't got time for daft games, lad.'

I told them about Jean's stolen ring and Colin's badge. About how we'd left them where we found them and made sure we didn't touch anything without gloves on so we wouldn't contaminate the evidence. Then I gave them the address of Scarface's bedsit.

They wanted Karwana's address too, to check things out with him.

'It looks like you've been roughed up pretty bad,' said Sergeant Bream, looking at the dried blood around my nose.

'He tried to strangle me,' I said. 'Karwana managed to stop him with a saucepan.'

The policemen went outside to radio in. They asked me and Jean to wait at the hostel.

The clock on the wall kept on ticking through the minutes. Me and Jean ran out of things to say. The police had been outside ages and there was still no sign of them.

'They don't believe us,' said Jean.

Stephen brought us both a cup of tea.

'Wow,' he said when he saw my drawing on the table. 'That's amazing.'

'He's a brilliant artist,' said Jean. 'He can draw anything.'

'My brother could draw like this,' he said, and winked at me.

I felt bad I'd felt nasty towards my own uncle when he'd kept looking at me, before. Now he was keeping our secret safe until we could talk properly.

It was nearly an hour before the policemen came back into the hostel and sat down with us again. Uncle Stephen left the room.

'Our colleagues have located the bedsit you told us about, Kieran,' Sergeant Bream said. 'They have apprehended a somewhat dazed man there.'

'Scarface,' I said.

DC Bream coughed.

'His real name is Jason Bryant. A local loan-shark already known to us, who preys on vulnerable people,' he said. 'He lost his temper when our officers asked him about Colin's death. He assumed we had a witness, claimed Colin fell in the water when he tried to snatch his bag from him to get an overdue payment. Says it wasn't his fault Colin couldn't swim.'

'Murdering toerag,' Jean said, again.

Sergeant Bream scowled at me. 'You and I need to have a chat about things, young man,' he said. 'Although you've managed to uncover some information that's very relevant to our current investigations, you can't just go around barging into people's homes and carrying out unofficial searches.'

'I know,' I said, looking at the table. 'But the door was open and I'd seen him attacking Jean when he stole her ring.'

He pressed his lips into a tight, straight line. 'Bryant gave us some other, very interesting information we

215

need to follow up on as a matter of urgency,' he said. 'Are your parents at home?'

I felt my face flush red.

'Mum and Tony don't know what's happened,' I said. 'Why do you need to speak to them?'

My heart hammered inside my chest. Tony was going to go mental when the police told him I'd grassed up his visitor, Scarface. I didn't want to go back to the house, ever.

Jean touched my hand and looked at the policemen.

'Things can be difficult for him at home,' she said, but they were busy writing stuff down.

Everything was ruined. When the police had gone away again and there was just me left, Tony would do something really, really bad. He would hurt me and Mum.

'I need the toilet,' I said, and stood up.

'Don't take too long,' Sergeant Bream said. 'We've got other crimes that need solving too. We've no plans to be here all night.'

I walked out of the small, stuffy office and back into the big room. Everybody out there looked up, waiting for me to say something but I just kept my head down and headed for the door.

I heard Stephen shouting me over but I just carried on walking. I didn't want my uncle-secret being ruined by screaming arguments back at the house.

I thought about what Tony would do to me if the police took me home. He would definitely think I'd grassed him up about Tyson. He would be very angry with me and Mum.

My heart squeezed inwards on itself, until it felt tight and small.

The cool, damp air stuck in my throat when I got outside. I wished I could sick up all the worries. Most of all, I wished I could run without stopping all the way back to the hospital, to see Grandma.

'Kieran!'

I glanced back and saw one of the policemen stepping out of the hostel entrance.

I started to walk really fast. Then faster. Until I was running and dodging into the back streets, where they couldn't catch me.

If they think I've run away, maybe they won't go to the house and speak to Tony, I told myself. If I can get back home first, I can whisper to Mum about what happened and we can get out of the house.

I didn't want any more trouble.

And, more than anything, I didn't want Tony to hurt Mum because of what I'd done.

39

SECRETS AND LIES

The policemen didn't follow me home, so I thought everything would be OK.

It was not OK.

When I turned the corner of the street, there were two police cars already outside our house.

I stood for a moment to think. I had my notebook and sketchpad. I had my letter and photograph from Martin Brunt at Sky News. I even had my pencil box. I knew where Grandma was, so I didn't have to go back into the house – I could run away for good.

And then I remembered.

Mum was in there.

I crept along the path at the side of the house and peered round the corner, through the back kitchen window.

There were a bunch of policemen in the kitchen. It was the first time I'd seen Tony and Ryan looking scared. Mum stood in the corner, her back pressed against the wall like she'd been glued to it.

The back door was half open and I could hear Tony saying, 'I've told you, I'm *clean*. I don't know even know a Jason Bryant.' He turned and glared at Mum. 'Well, tell them, woman, don't just bleeping stand there.'

My mum opened her mouth to speak and then closed it again.

'For God's sake, back me up!' His eyes narrowed at her and I could see his knuckles gleaming white through the skin stretched tight above them.

I wanted to turn round and run but I could never leave my mum.

I squeezed in the kitchen behind the uniforms and shut the door behind me.

I'm not supposed to go in the kitchen when visitors come but I really wanted to see the policemen up close. They looked tougher than Sergeant Bream. I wished I had one of their belts with all the cop-stuff hanging down from it.

'Get out,' Tony said, and clenched his teeth together. His eyes were darting about. Ryan stood in the hall doorway. He looked pale and stared at the floor.

I felt brave with the policemen there.

'I want to stay with Mum,' I said.

Tony pointed straight at me. 'I said out, retard.'

'That's not a very nice way to speak to him, Tony,' one of the policeman said, smiling at me. 'He looks a nice enough lad. What's your name, son?'

'Kieran,' I said, looking at his belt. There were some impressive things on there that could stop Tony in his tracks if he lunged for me.

Tony was staring at me really hard. He didn't say anything but I knew the words in his head were, *Get out, retard. Get out.*

My mum looked down at the floor. Her bony fingers pulled and twisted against each other. She looked thin and small next to Tony's big, podgy frame.

I didn't move.

'You look like a helpful lad,' the policeman said, patting his belt. 'Maybe we can ask you a few questions.'

'No way!' Tony was really mad with the policeman now. He looked mad at me too. 'You're not allowed to talk to him. You can see he's not right in the head. Nothing he says means anything.'

'Miss Crane says you should help the police if you can,' I said.

'It's a pity everybody around here doesn't think that,' said one of the policemen, and the other uniforms laughed. Tony and Ryan didn't join in.

'Kieran looks a smart lad,' the first policeman said. It seemed to me like he was in charge. 'We're just asking your dad and brother a few questions.'

'They're not my real dad and brother,' I said.

I could see the top of the baton. It was in its own leather sheath with a press-stud fastening. When he turned to say something to one of the others, I saw the handcuffs.

'So . . .' The policeman talked slower and louder than

before. He was talking to Tony but looking at me. 'You don't sell drugs from this house, Tony?'

The policeman was trying to gain my confidence so I would tell him what he wanted to know. It was a well-known way of getting information that I'd seen on *CSI*.

Sometimes, when they got what they wanted, the police just left the scene. It meant that if I told them what I knew, they might leave, and then me and Mum would have to face Tony on our own.

Then one of the other policemen said, 'I wonder if anyone has seen people come to the door and give money to Tony in exchange for stuff? That would help us a lot.'

'*Bleep! Bleep! Bleep!*' yelled Tony.

I knew exactly why Tony didn't want to tell the police about his visitors, but I wasn't supposed to say anything. I remembered all the times Tony had zipped up his mouth at me and made his hands into fist-shapes.

The head policeman looked at me.

'What's in there?' I pointed to a closed pouch on his belt.

'This?' He opened the pouch and pulled something out. 'This is a flashlight, Kieran. It helps us see when it's dark or find things that are hidden.'

He looked at Tony, with his mouth set in a mean, pinched line.

'Where are the rocks, Tony?'

'I don't know what you're talking about,' Tony said. He didn't look scared any more.

'We haven't got a clue what you're talking about, right, Dad?' I heard a quiver in Ryan's voice. He was trying to smile, to show he wasn't scared, but he just looked silly.

'That's right. We're no wiser than the retard over there,' Tony said, grinning.

For a few seconds the room went quiet.

Then something amazing happened.

My mum stopped twisting her fingers and looked up from the floor.

'His name is *Kieran*.'

Her voice was quiet and a bit shaky but we all looked at her.

'What did you say?' Tony was using his warning voice. The one that sounded quiet and calm but meant he was really, really mad.

All the colour had leaked out of Mum's face, apart from two pink spots in the middle of her cheeks. She never answered Tony back.

'He's my son . . . and his name is Kieran,' she said. 'Don't call him a retard.'

'You . . .' Tony took a step towards her, even though the police were there.

My mind filled with a flood of pictures.

My mum's bruised face.

Tyson's starved body.

Spending night after night upstairs, alone in my room.

Someone had to stop Tony hurting people and getting away with it.

I dodged out of the kitchen to the understairs cupboard.

'Kieran, come back!' I heard the policeman shout.

I moved the vacuum cleaner and pulled up the rug.

I grabbed the toolbox from under the floorboards and dashed back into the kitchen with it.

'This is what you're looking for,' I said.

'Shut the—' Tony jumped towards me and the policemen all jumped on him. Another held Ryan's arms behind his back. 'He doesn't know anything!'

But I did know.

I knew so much more than they thought.

'The drugs are in little bags in here,' I said, shaking the toolbox. 'Both their fingerprints will be all over the stuff. Forensics will have no trouble finding them.'

Mum stood with her hands covering her mouth looking at the toolbox.

'What's this? You've been selling drugs from the house – from our home?'

'They come when you're at work, Mum,' I said.

'Are you saying you knew nothing about this?' the head policeman said to Mum.

Tony gave a hard, wicked laugh.

'Are you joking? Neither of them know anything about my *business deals*,' he spat. 'They're both thick as pig-muck. Like mother, like son.'

I took a deep breath and said the words quickly so I couldn't change my mind.

'The definition of "stupid" is giving the police a full confession without even realizing you've done it.'

Tony's face turned puce and he made to take a step towards me before my words sank in and the colour drained from his cheeks.

'Very useful, sir,' said one of the policemen, brandishing handcuffs and grinning. 'Why don't you come down to the station and tell us more about your "business deals", eh?'

'I haven't done anything wrong,' Ryan mumbled, backing into the hallway. 'He made me fill the bags; I didn't know what the stuff was.'

'You're nearly seventeen years old, son,' said the first policeman, frowning. 'Pull the other one.'

The whole kitchen erupted into a sea of thrashing arms and hands as the police surrounded Tony and Ryan. I shuffled along the wall and stood next to Mum and she reached for my hand and held it tight. When I looked up at her face, her eyes were squeezed shut but tears were still spilling down her cheeks.

Ryan just stood quietly and let them cuff him. He

looked over at me once but his eyes were wide and glazed, not glaring and mad.

Tony was screaming so loud, I couldn't even understand what he was saying.

But I wasn't even scared of his noise any more.

Mum and I stood back as the police carted Tony, kicking and screaming, out of the door. Only one policeman escorted Ryan. He was crying like a little boy.

I felt a knot in my stomach. I wondered if me and Ryan could've been friends if Tony had let me teach him how to draw.

'Wait,' Ryan said, when he got to the door. He mumbled something to the policeman, who looked around Ryan's back and reached up to feel along the top of one of the kitchen cupboards.

He looked at what was in his hand and looked at Ryan.

'Give it to him,' said Ryan, nodding.

I held out my hand and the policeman dropped something into it.

'I'm sorry,' he said, starting to cry again.

Then the policeman walked him out of the house.

I looked down at my open hand. It was the missing sharpener from my pencil box.

(40)

SMART

Miss Crane always says that a good story should have a beginning, a middle and an end. The beginning was when I found Colin's body in the river. The middle was when Tony lost his job and started having his visitors. This next bit is the end.

The nurses had taken all the tubes and pipes away and Grandma sat propped up with pillows, in bed.

'So, Tony and Ryan were arrested and taken away by the police?' she said, sipping her tea.

I nodded. Uncle Stephen had dropped me and Mum off at the hospital and I got to tell Grandma all the details.

'Tony was swearing and fighting back, but the policemen just flipped him into the yard like a rag doll.'

'And Ryan?'

'He was sad,' I said. 'The policeman said he might have to go to a young offenders' institute for a while because he knew full well what he was doing when he helped his dad.'

'Serves him right,' said Grandma, 'the way he treated you.'

I wrapped my hand round the pencil sharpener in my pocket.

'I think he was as scared of Tony as I was,' I said quietly.

The nurse wrote something down on her clipboard.

'You're doing well, Gladys,' she said. 'Looks like you'll be home in a day or so.'

I could tell Mum was happy about that, even though she'd been really quiet since Tony's arrest at the house.

Grandma reached over and touched Mum's hand.

'Everything is going to be fine.'

Mum nodded.

'Where has your voice gone, Mum?' I asked her, when the nurse had left. 'You're hardly saying anything.'

Mum didn't answer.

'They've already allocated me a new council house, so start packing,' Grandma said. She was trying to fill the quiet spaces with good thoughts.

Grandma meant that we were going to live with her again, like we did before Tony.

The bed-and-breakfast Uncle Stephen had paid for us to stay in was tiny and we had to share the bathroom with other people, including the man upstairs who left wee on the seat.

I had to get the bus to school each day. Still, it was tons better than living with Tony and Ryan.

I looked at Mum. She looked small, like a little lost bird, sitting in the chair.

'Will it be OK?' I asked Grandma again.

'It will,' Grandma answered. 'Your mum is going to be my carer and you'll concentrate on getting top grades at school so you can work for the *Evening Post*, like you've always dreamed.'

The words sounded great, but the feelings in my tummy didn't match.

Grandma said maybe Jean and Karwana could come over to the new house for a drink to celebrate our new start. Everything in our lives was suddenly different but it didn't even feel like it was real yet.

I got spiky jabs of excitement when I thought about the weekend. Uncle Stephen was going to pick me up and take me to his house to meet my new cousin, Bradley.

Things were getting better but it was still taking a long time.

I looked over at Mum.

'Why are you sad?' I said.

'Honestly, I'm OK, Kieran,' she sighed. 'Stop worrying.'

It was Mum that looked the most worried, not me. I don't know why because Tony had gone. The police even told Mum that Tony wouldn't get bail as he had 'previous'. That means he's already got a police record.

'Things will be OK,' I said.

I wasn't one hundred per cent sure about this, but I

did a good job of sounding like it. I hoped it would help Mum if she was feeling a bit scared.

Mum didn't answer.

'Sometimes, people think they need somebody else to make it in this life.' Grandma winked at me. 'But you have to remember that the one person you can truly always rely on is yourself.'

'You can rely on me too, Mum,' I said.

I leaned over and gave my mum a hug. I didn't even feel like a statue.

'I know,' she said, and smiled again. This time it was a real one.

I closed my eyes and painted a picture of the moment, in my mind.

All the matchstick people in this painting were good. Nobody was running in different directions and there was no one to call me dumb or hurt my mum any more.

Laurence Stephen Lowry once said, *You don't need brains to paint, just feelings.*

I know exactly what he meant.

I was going to paint some brilliant pictures with my new feelings.

After Tony and Ryan had been taken away, I showed the policeman the list of car registrations I'd copied down in my notebook and all the sketches I'd done of some of Tony's visitors.

He said I was the smartest kid he'd ever met.

ACKNOWLEDGEMENTS

I'd like to give special thanks to my fantastic agent, Clare Wallace, for her enthusiasm and belief in my writing, her invaluable advice and her never-ending support.

Also, a massive thank you to Rachel Kellehar, my editor at Macmillan Children's Books, for her amazing insight, her genuine love of *Smart* and for being such a pleasure to work with.

In addition, I would like to thank each and every one of Darley's Angels at the Darley Anderson Literary Agency for everything they do, particularly Mary Darby, and Vicki le Feuvre for her truly excellent editorial insight and inexhaustible ideas.

Likewise, thank you to the entire MCB team, who are so professional and innovative in their ideas, and especially to publicity manager Catherine Alport, and to the whole of the Design team, who did such an amazing job on the cover.

Last, but never least, my love and thanks go out to my family for their unshakeable belief in me and their love and support. Mackie, Francesca and Mama, you three have shared my writing roller-coaster and I couldn't have done it without you.